# KEEPING SECRETS

*Recent Titles by Cynthia Harrod-Eagles from Severn House*

A CORNISH AFFAIR
DANGEROUS LOVE
DIVIDED LOVE
EVEN CHANCE
LAST RUN
NOBODY'S FOOL
PLAY FOR LOVE
A RAINBOW SUMMER

# KEEPING SECRETS

## Cynthia Harrod-Eagles

This title first published in Great Britain 1998 by
SEVERN HOUSE PUBLISHERS LTD of
9–15 High Street, Sutton, Surrey SM1 1DF.
Parts of this work were originally published in
Paperback format only in 1983 under the title
*The Unfinished* and pseudonym of *Elizabeth Bennett*.
First published in the USA 1998 by
SEVERN HOUSE PUBLISHERS INC., of
595 Madison Avenue, New York, NY 10022.

British Library Cataloguing in Publication Data

Harrod-Eagles,  Cynthia
         Keeping Secrets
         1.   Love stories
         1.   Title  II. Bennett,  Elizabeth
         823.9'14 [F]

         ISBN 0-7278-5388-0

Typeset by Hewer Text Ltd.,
Edinburgh, Scotland.
Printed and bound in Great Britain by
MPG Books Ltd, Bodmin, Cornwall.

# AUTHOR'S NOTE

This novel is one of those which first appeared under the pen-name of Elizabeth Bennett. In reissuing them under my own name, Severn House has asked me to explain how they came to be written.

People sometimes ask me if I always wanted to be a writer, and the truthful answer is that I always *was* a writer – in the sense that I always wrote. Short stories, poems, essays – anything would do, as long as I was putting words together and 'telling the tale'. When all else failed, or there was no paper (it was still in short supply in my childhood), I carried on a running narrative inside my head about an orphan girl who lived in a cave in the mountains and was befriended by wild animals.

When I reached the grand old age of ten, I began writing my first full-length novel, about an orphan girl who tamed a wild pony (I had two perfectly good parents of my own, and can't imagine why I kept writing about orphans!). When it was finished I began a sequel, and then another. In all I wrote about nine children's novels over my teenage years, and even sent some off to publishers, but they were always rejected, though very kindly.

I went to university and went off ponies a bit when I discovered boys. The result was my first adult novel, which again I submitted to a publisher and had rejected. I changed universities, wrote another adult novel, submitted it – and to my utter astonishment won the Young Writer's Award for it. I had never really believed I would ever be published, but that had never stopped me writing. Now I held my first published novel, *The Waiting Game*, in my hand, for the first time. It was a wonderful moment. However, I still had to work for a living, and with a full-time office job, writing had to be squeezed into my evenings and weekends. What happened next was that I was asked by a publisher to write a series of modern romances for them, to order, and in receiving my first commission I felt I had taken an important step in becoming a proper, professional writer. The result was the Emma Woodhouse novels.

Why did I use a pseudonym? Was I ashamed to put my own name on them? Not at all; but in those days publishers believed that if you wrote more than one kind of novel, you had to have a different name for each kind. I was asked to choose a pen-name, and since I happened to be in the middle of my annual re-reading of all the Jane Austen novels, I chose Emma Woodhouse after the heroine of *Emma*. When later another, different publisher commissioned me to write some romances about 'career-girls', I was obliged to choose another pen-name, and this time, since I was reading *Pride and Prejudice*, I chose the name of Elizabeth Bennett.

In course of time the Emma Woodhouse and Elizabeth Bennett books sold out and went out of print, and they have lain dormant ever since. But when I won the Romantic Novelists' Association Novel of Year Award for my book *Emily*, Severn House thought that perhaps my readers might like the chance to see these early works of mine. So here they are, reissued without disguise. I am very glad to see them again in this handsome new edition, proudly flying the banner of my own name this time, and I do hope that you enjoy reading them as much as I enjoyed writing them.

*Cynthia Harrod-Eagles, 1998*

# ONE

'Annie, you really must be mad,' Julie said, staring at her sister across the kitchen. 'Stark, staring mad. What are you doing – practising for International Year of the Masochist?'

Annabel, sitting on the corner of the kitchen table and fiddling with the cutlery, shrugged.

'I mean, after all you've been through –' Julie began again, and Annie looked up in irritation.

'All right,' she interrupted. 'Don't go on. I know what I've been through.'

'After all you've been through,' Julie repeated, undeterred – nothing ever made Julie swerve from a course she'd chosen, verbal or physical – 'to step straight back into the fire –'

'I should have thought,' Annie said with cold sarcasm, 'that it would be obvious even to you that this is not the same orchestra.'

'It's still an orchestra,' Julie said as if pointing out some simple logic.

'Orchestras work fourteen hours a day, seven days a week, fifty weeks a year. Don't you think the best way to avoid meeting someone from one orchestra would be to spend your time with another one? When did you ever go to a concert where two orchestras were playing at once?'

Julie changed positions. 'It's bound to remind you, pet,' she said gently. Annie turned her head away slightly, as if avoiding an undesired attention.

'I don't need reminding. I'm not likely to forget.'

'And anyway,' Julie changed positions yet again, 'it's such a menial sort of job, for someone with your talents.' Annie regarded her elder sister washing smalls in the sink with a sardonic eye, but she refrained from pointing out that Julie's life was spent doing tasks even more menial, and for no pay. Nothing was ever to be gained from attempting to persuade a married woman that she would have done better not to

5

marry. 'I mean, orchestral attendant!' Julie shook her head sadly, and then stared out of the window, striking a casual pose. Annabel knew what was coming next. 'Why don't you try playing again?'

'Now, Julie,' Annie began warningly, but Julie rushed on eagerly now she had made a beginning.

'I know, I know, but couldn't you just try? You haven't touched it for years, and I'm sure if you just practised for a few weeks it would come back to you –'

'I'll never play again,' Annie said. Her face was bleak now, and she avoided her sister's eyes. 'I've told you that. It's gone. I can't play. I don't want to talk about it.'

'It seems terrible to let him ruin your life like that,' Julie said. 'I mean as well as all the other ways he hurt you – if I were you –' She let the sentence peter out. If you were me, Annie thought, I'd probably be you, and married to Pat, and I'd like that even less than being me. Julie squeezed out the rinsed clothes and threw them into a plastic bowl. 'There,' she said, 'that's that done. I'll hang them out in a minute. But, honestly, Annie, isn't there anything else you can do? It does seem to me a retrograde step.'

'I'm not qualified for anything else,' Annie said. 'All I know how to do – all I *knew* how to do,' she corrected herself ruefully, 'was play. I know music, and that's all. There isn't any other job I could take. And at least I know a bit about an orchestra's routine. And I'll travel around, and meet people. That's better than frowsting in some dreadful office or shop all my life, isn't it?'

'Good gracious, I hope you don't think of working all your life? You'll get married –' Julie began.

'Married!' Annie interrupted with a derisive snort. Julie looked hurt.

'It's the best thing for a woman,' she said.

'Which woman?' Annie countered. 'All right, I know you're happy. You love Pat and he loves you and everything in the garden's lovely. But look at all the other marriages that don't work, and all the women who are miserable because they spend their lives chasing love and marriage in

6

vain. Better to chase a job you've some chance of succeeding at. I'm no good with men. I think I must be a born mistress, and you're a born wife. I don't know anyone whose socks *I'd* be willing to wash.'

'Not even Geoffrey's?' Julie asked slyly, and then wished she hadn't, for Annie still could not hear his name without pain.

'Not even Geoffrey's,' Annie said, her gaze steady, and her mouth quirking with an acknowledgment that it *was* funny, in a way. 'I'd have died for him without hesitation, but he would have had to wash his own bloody socks. Anyway, all the people I'll be meeting from now on will be musicians, and you wouldn't want me to marry a musician, now would you?' she finished wheedlingly.

'All the more reason for not taking on this stupid job,' Julie said, but she had given up the fight. She and Annie were alike in their stubbornness if in nothing else. When they were younger, people had never believed they were sisters, not looking beyond the obvious differences of colouring – Julie was dark and Annie was fair. Julie had been the noisy, extrovert sister, quick-tempered, rather aggressive, good at games at school and always sure of what she wanted and where she was going. Annabel had been quiet, a dreamy, introverted child, not given to either saying or doing much, until her musical ability blossomed. But in her quiet way, she had always been as determined to get what she wanted as Julie had, and they had quarrelled frequently and violently through their years of growing up together, Julie shouting and throwing things, Annie stonewalling with an obstinate lip jutting out.

But they had remained friends despite that, and now that Julie had what she wanted – her husband, children, and big new bungalow on a nice estate – she was anxious to see Annie settled as comfortably. She often urged Annie to come and stay there, even to live there permanently, for she reasoned that she would be able to find Annie the right man and get her settled down and married in no time. Annie resisted. She did not want to be *settled down*, especially not with anyone

7

Julie was likely to introduce her to – friends of Pat's and people who lived on the estate – and she had a very cogent reason for not wanting to come and live at Kerriton (the name of the bungalow). The reason was Pat himself.

Outside a dog barked. 'There's Pat now,' Julie said, and as if conjured by her words the stiff back door groaned and jerked open, and there Pat was, the man coming home, bringing with him a breath of the outside world, and the old-knife smell of a day in the sweat and grime of a city office and the long crowded journey home. He greeted Julie casually – 'Hello, love!' – and grinned at Annie. 'Hello, li'l sis. You here?'

'Hello, big bro',' she replied in kind. He was a big man, broad and fair and ruddy-skinned, with mild, surprised blue eyes. She went across to him and turned her face up to be kissed, pushing her chest out provocatively. Close to she felt the power of his big maleness, smelled his rank man-smell. It was a thing you either liked or didn't, as horse lovers relish the smell of horses. He stooped towards her, and at the last moment she flicked her head an inch to one side and his kiss landed on her cheek and only the corner of her mouth. As he turned away, his meaty hand brushed against her left breast – accidentally.

It was a game they played, of tormenting each other, of testing their sexuality against each other as one might test a blade against the thumb, knowing that if it really was sharp they could be hurt – but it was only a game. It began before Pat and Julie were even married. They had been engaged for a few weeks before Annabel even met him, for she had been away on tour (that was in the days when she was still playing) all summer. She met him at a party given by a friend of the family, and she remembered still the moment when she had first seen him, when their eyes had met across the room and they had exchanged the curious stare of recognition that passes between two sexually attractive people – a stare that says, *I know you; you are like me.*

Later in the evening, when they had both got rather drunk, she went out into the garden for a breath of air, and he had

8

followed her, catching up with her in the gloom of a neglected shrubbery. Without saying a word he had taken hold of her and they had kissed, a long, interested, friendly kiss, full of sex and questions. Then he had let her go, leaving one hand resting on her shoulder as if to restrain her, regarding her with the slightly fuddled gravity of the half-cut.

'So you're going to be my sister,' he said.

'So it seems,' she replied. He sighed heavily.

'Oh well, that's the way it goes. Pity we didn't meet before.' He kissed her again, and then made a slow and careful way back indoors. She knew what he meant – not that he had chosen the 'wrong sister' as in magazine stories, but that it would have been nice for them to have had sex together, and now they were as good as related it was too late.

'Annie's got a new job,' Julie told him as she carried a tray to the door. 'Tell him about it, Annie, while I take Mother's tea up.' That was Pat's mother, bed-ridden and senile, whom Julie looked after good-humouredly and uncomplainingly – another evidence of how different the sisters were. Annie couldn't imagine doing *that* for anyone, either.

Pat dragged out a chair from under the kitchen table and sat down heavily, tired from the day at work. His great muscled thighs seemed ready to burst the seams of his dark city suit. Annie always thought he looked odd in clothes, like an animal dressed up; he ought to be seen in nothing but a swimming-clout or a loin-cloth at most – his body didn't seem to fit his profession in the least.

'Tell us then, Annie,' he said. Annabel found herself moving about the room restlessly at this second exposition of how she had applied for and been given the job of orchestral attendant to the Metropolitan Symphony Orchestra, or Met Symf, or MSO, almost as if she felt guilty about it. In contrast, Pat sat massively still, his pale blue gaze never shifting from her face until she had finished. Then he stretched and sighed, and said,

'Do you think it's the right thing to do?'

9

Annie only shrugged. She could say a lot to Pat with a shrug, and this one said: don't badger me – I don't know if it's wrong or right, but it's a thing to do, and anything is better than doing nothing.

'It doesn't sound like a job with much opportunity or prospects. Bit of a dead end, isn't it?'

Annie said, 'I'm not qualified for anything.' Now he shrugged.

'There are things you can do without being qualified. But you know that isn't the point.'

'Then what is?' she asked defiantly. He forced her to meet his eyes.

'You're wasting yourself,' he said.

'Oh –' another shrug, which meant: I am unhappy, I have been hurt, I don't care about myself, I want to punish myself for being able to be hurt.

'Why don't you start playing again?'

'I can't,' she said flatly. 'I want to get away from that question. How long before people stop asking it? I just want to get away.'

He nodded, understanding, but neither condoning nor condemning. There was a lot Annie liked about Pat, and one of the things was his neutrality, his ability to be detached about things, even things that closely concerned him. It was something that Julie couldn't understand, and many a time she was driven almost to gibbering fury by her inability to make *him* lose his head.

The evening went its accustomed way. They had a meal, a few drinks, talked, played cards. Pat went to see his mother, to look in on the sleeping babies, and at ten-thirty he got up to drive Annie home.

'Won't be long, love,' he said, kissing Julie, and stretched out a big paw towards Annabel. 'Come on, Skinny Lizzie, let's be having you.' It was all carefully calculated double-entendre, and as she allowed her hand to be engulfed by his she felt his squeeze it and nudge her palm with a finger. It was about a twenty-minute drive, and they did it in silence, but Annie knew he hadn't spoken his last word on the subject.

10

He drew up outside Annie's flat, turned off the engine and doused the lights and sat for a moment, lost in thought. Then he gave a tiny grunt, as of one who has made up his mind about something, and swivelling himself in his seat he drew her into his arms and kissed her, no brotherly kiss this, but tongue and teeth and purpose.

She was slightly dizzy when he lifted his mouth from hers at last and cradled her head on his shoulder, stroking her hair kindly. He sighed.

'Hmm, that was nice,' he said. 'What a pity about us.' She gave a little snorting laugh. 'Don't laugh,' he said. 'One day –'

'One day, nuts,' she said. He laughed too, and kissed her forehead.

'You're right,' he said. She pulled herself free and sat up, automatically straightening her hair and collar. 'All the same,' he said, suddenly serious, 'you're wrong about the job. It won't answer, you know.'

She looked at him apprehensively.

'It's only running away,' he said. 'You're running away from your own tail. It comes with you wherever you go. You forgave him – why won't you forgive yourself?'

'Running away?' she said. 'I wouldn't have thought you could call this direction running *away*.'

'It isn't the direction that matters – it's the running. You had a bad time – okay; but it's *over*. No one can make you unhappy – or happy. You have to make yourself.'

'Do you think I shouldn't take the job?'

He shrugged. 'It doesn't matter. Take it, if you like, but *use* it. Make yourself a life. Put yourself around a bit. You shouldn't be wasting your lovely body on your fat old brother-in-law.'

She laughed. 'I love you.'

'Who doesn't?' he said modestly. 'All right, that's enough homespun philosophy for one evening. Get your gorgeous arse out of my car and let me go home to bed. Night night. Sweet dreams.'

'Good night. And thanks,' she said, getting out.

11

'Balls,' he said amiably, and they went their separate ways.

Annie arrived at the hall on her first day at nine-thirty, and skirted the great green pantechnicon with the orchestra's name in gold script along the side, which was pulled up alongside the artists' entrance. At the rear of it two men were lifting out the last of the double-basses, and as she paused to watch them one flicked a wink at her and the other whistled.

'Oy-oy!' they chorused cheerfully, and 'Which one of 'em are *you* after, then?'

'All of them,' Annie replied, smiling. They paused, considering this. One was tall and thin and young, the other short and wiry, balding and middle-aged; but they were alike in their automatically-assumed expression of lechery, which all 'roadies' or 'humpers' seemed to wear. The younger one finally pronounced in a Scottish accent,

'I get it! You're the new OA – am I right?' Annie nodded.

'Well you're an improvement on the old one,' the other added, looking her up and down. ' 'is tits 'ad started sagging. What would your name be, then?' Annie told him. The young man balanced a bass on its end and held out a hand politely for her to shake.

'I'm Tam, an' he's Benny,' he said, and flicked his head towards his mate. 'Some folks canna tell us apart, but if you remember that I'm the handsome one, an' he's the ol' bastard, you'll be okay. An' never accept an invitation from Benny to tak a look at his Stradivarius.'

'I'll remember that helpful advice,' Annie laughed. Benny looked sour and spat expertly sideways into the road.

'Yeah, well, when you two've quite finished desiccating my character, perhaps we can get on wiv a bit of work. Otherwise we'll have the fairy-bleeding-prince flapping round us.'

This, Annie recognised, was a reference to the man from whom she was taking over, the previous orchestral attendant, Tony Taper, known usually as Tiny Tony, or even Tiny

12

Tim. He met her now as she came out of the lift into the backstage area, and fluttered over to shake her hand, an hysterical elf of a man, five-feet-nothing of permanent anxiety. Annie, shaking his miniscule hand and smiling at him from the top of her five-foot-three body felt like the Jolly Green Giant by comparison.

'You'd better come and be introduced to the chaps,' he said. 'Not that they're all here yet, but those that are – of course, that'll be one of your jobs, to round them up for rehearsals. Some of them never arrive on time, and some of them cut things so fine. The conductors – Bennett, for instance, doesn't mind if people slip on to the platform after he's started, but Rostrovitch goes completely *mad*! And you'll have to watch the brass – if they aren't playing in the first few bars they won't turn up until they think they're wanted. I'm *always* trying to get the chaps to be here and ready five minutes before time, but they just laugh. Perhaps you'll have better luck with them.'

He looked at her doubtfully as he said it, unable to imagine she would have any more influence over eighty individuals than he had had.

'It isn't all chaps, is it?' Annie said. 'You have some women players?'

'Only five at the moment,' Taper said. 'But they're no trouble. Perhaps you'd like to come and meet them first. At least I always know where *they* are.'

The women members of the MSO were sitting in the orchestra's bar drinking coffee and talking – three violins, one cello, and a flute. The latter was called Miss Piggy behind her back because she had developed flautist's lip to an alarming degree. They looked up at Annie with cool interest as Taper introduced them all round, and smiled politely at her.

'I hope the Board know what they're doing, introducing a decorative young thing like you to this band of lechers, dear,' said the eldest of the violins, a woman called Walker. She was a stout, motherly-shaped woman with a splendid beehive of hennaed hair and the hefty quivering arms of a washerwoman, but she was in fact the principal of the second-violin section, and Annie was forced to consider yet again how talent came in all sorts of unlikely shapes and sizes. 'Poor Tony had a bad enough time – but just you be firm with them, dear, and if they give you any trouble, just come to me. Many's a time I've had to put one of them in his place. They don't argue with *me*, dear, I can tell you.' She nodded with quiet confidence, and Annie smiled her thanks. As she and Taper were walking away, Mrs Walker called after her,

'And don't let that Warren Stacker sweet-talk you, dear. Charm in its worst form!'

That was the name of the orchestra's leader, Annie knew. Taper looked worried. 'Don't take any notice of Doris,' he murmured to Annie anxiously. 'She and Warren have never got on. He thinks she's too bossy and he won't play up to her like the others. I'd better introduce you to him next.'

Annie knew at once, however, what Mrs Walker had meant, for Warren Stacker was smooth, suave, well dressed and had the kind of dazzling smile that seemed more full of teeth than the normal person's. He held her hand rather too long after shaking it, and gazed into her eyes in a way that was meant to make her melt. He had not long ago joined the MSO from an American orchestra, and had a slight American accent, which Annie thought unforgiveable when she discovered shortly afterwards that he had only been in the States for eighteen months.

'I'm sure you're going to love being with us,' he cooed like the host of a television show. 'Is Tony taking you round? That's marvellous. I'd better come along with you, put my seal of approval on things.' Which might have been a joke, except that it wasn't.

So Taper and Warren Stacker introduced her to as many more of the members as was possible before the rehearsal was due to start. Mostly she met with pleasant smiles and interested looks. Some she had met before – they were the members of the orchestra's Board, which was recruited from its ranks, plus a couple of players she had met subbing at other concerts. Some gave her lecherous looks and cracked lewd jokes. One, the orchestra's resident queer, gave her a look of disgust; and one, the principal horn-player Ivor Hotchkiss, though he spoke with distant politeness, stared at her with dislike and disapproval. Annie wondered what axe he had to grind, but neither of her companions offered any explanation, and she kept quiet, deciding that whatever it was would be made clear soon enough.

Before the introductions were half over, it was time for the rehearsal to start, and Tony Taper was flying about on his little pointed toes clapping his hands and clucking after the men like an anguished hen.

'Come along please! Come along *please*! Ted, Andy, David – *do* hurry up. And where's Frank? Has anyone seen Frank yet? Come along, chaps!'

A languidly elegant oboist strolled past unhurriedly, murmuring 'Come along please it's time. Come along please it's time,' which Annie recognised as a quotation from T. S. Eliot. As he caught her eye, he gave a ghostly wink and added softly, 'I had not thought death had undone so many!' which was another. Annie added it to her mental notes. It was useful to have a handle to begin an acquaintance.

Once the players had all been chivvied on to the platform and the rehearsal had begun, Tony Taper relaxed slightly and talked to Annie about the rest of her duties in a more normal tone of voice. It was only towards the end of the rehearsal that they had time to slip into the auditorium and watch and listen. Annie looked at the people on the platform with amusement. It was hard to imagine that these un-shaven, sloppily-dressed yawners were the same people as the dedicated musicians who would appear immaculate – at least from a distance – in evening dress at the evening's concert. How little would the audience know when they applauded their elegant heroes! – there was the timpanist reading the share index in the *Financial Times*; the lead trumpet showing his holiday snaps to the second trumpet; the tuba-player wading his way through *War and Peace*; one of the back cellists furtively hunting up his favourites in that day's *Pink 'un* during rests.

As a child Annabel had been taken to concerts by her father, and had seen the far-off figures of the musicians like so many gods on the lower slopes of Olympus. This illusion had persisted into her teenage years, and when one of these gods had condescended to speak to her one day outside a concert hall, she had been as shocked and delighted as if the Queen herself had phoned up and invited her round to Buck House for a bit of hot supper. It had come as a tremendous shock to discover that the gods were human beings – but a fairly pleasant shock, all told.

The music stopped, the conductor dismissed the players, and Tony Taper was already on his feet and urging Annie to accompany him backstage to continue introductions.

'You were miles away,' he complained as Annie came to and rose to her towering height above him.

'I was just thinking how nice it was to be back,' she said. 'All the prognostications were wrong.'

Tony Taper did not understand that bit, but he didn't ask any questions. In his high-speed life there was never enough time even for the things he did understand, let alone any mysteries.

# TWO

'So this is the glamour, romance and sparkle your life in future will hold,' Pat said as he drove Annie and Julie through the quiet streets of Swansea towards the town hall for the evening's concert.

'Give it a chance,' Annie replied, unruffled by his sarcasm. 'The glamour will be arranged on a scale of increasing intensity. And you must admit that this –' waving a hand at the view of the sea, sparkling in the late sunshine, and the distant green of the hills around the bay – 'that this has it all ways up over Tesco's in Catford High Street.'

'You've never been to Catford,' Pat objected. 'For all you know it might be the Atlantic City, New Jersey, of the entire south-east.'

'You've never been to Atlantic City, New Jersey,' Annabel objected, recognising the beginning of a quotation from *Butch Cassidy and the Sundance Kid*. They had seen the film four times in all, and could quote almost the whole dialogue *ad lib*. The next line would have been 'I was *born* in Atlantic City, New Jersey,' but even as Pat was opening his mouth to say it, Julie, who had no memory for a quotation, broke in with, 'Are you two going to talk nonsense *all* night, or is there an interval?'

'Look at the nice scenery, dear,' Pat said kindly, patting her hand, 'and remember that tomorrow is another washing-day.'

'I must say, though,' Julie went on, ignoring him, 'that the job seems to be suiting you. You look much better already – more relaxed and happy.'

'In that case it must suit me better than the last person who did the job – he had to leave to have a heart attack,' Annie said. 'I do feel cheerful, though. Somehow it's good to be back, if you know what I mean. There's a special atmosphere about music-making, and I was missing it without realising

17

it.' Julie was evidently about to say something, but Annie caught her eye and stopped her. 'And the answer to that one is no. Don't push it, Julie darling. I can't play any more. The healing process stops there.'

'Actually,' Julie said, lying with dignity, 'I was only going to say isn't that the town hall over there?'

Pat caught Annie's eye in the driving mirror and they exchanged a smile of complicity.

'Yes,' Annie said. 'It's rather splendid, isn't it, with that big clock tower and all the green lawns all around? There was an American student at rehearsal this morning, and I went out on to the steps for a breath of fresh air and found him standing there admiring the view, and he waved a hand around at the lawns and said, "I love Britain – it looks so furtle". Pronounced that way it didn't sound at all like fertile. It sounded so funny.'

'Like a sort of *portmanteau* word,' Pat suggested. 'A furtle – a furtive fumble.'

'Very appropriate for the environs of the MSO,' Annie said drily. 'It's amazing how the groupies do hang around. Quite shocks the older members – and Percy.'

'Percy?' Julie queried.

'John King. Known as Percy. King is also a misnomer – he's the resident queer. Here we are again, then – back to the grind.' This as the car drew up alongside the steps of the town hall. 'I'll see you afterwards, at the party, shall I? You've got your tickets?'

'Yes – and the invitations. We'll just go for a stroll by the sea until the concert starts,' Pat said. 'And it had better be good.'

'Don't look a gift concert in the mouth – you didn't have to pay for the tickets,' Annie retorted.

'No, but it's a long way to come down here to listen to a load of old rubbish,' Pat said.

'Met Symf is not rubbish,' Annie protested. Pat winked at Julie.

'Fell for it, didn't she? All this languid carelessness is a pose – she's really devoted to them, singly and collectively.'

18

'Oh, go away and play tricks on someone else,' Annie said with mock exasperation. 'And no furtling in the back row during the concert!'

'Oh most beautiful, beloved, apple of my eye, goddess of love, of virtue, of wisdom –' the words, burbled in Annie's ear, were accompanied by a pair of hands around her waist with just a suggestion of creeping-upwards about them.

'All right, Angus, what is it this time?' she asked without turning round, so that he had to walk round her to face her. He pretended to be disappointed.

'You recognised me,' he said, and then brightened. 'Perhaps such instant recognition portends reciprocation –'

'Nope,' Annie cut him off briskly. 'It don't portend nuffink, except that I recognise the smell of Johnnie Walker Black Label when I sniff it.'

'At least I haven't been reduced to ameliorating my sobriety on inferior potables,' he said with ravishing dignity. Angus Mackie was the orchestra's second oboe, a small pale-faced Glaswegian with neat dark hair and large blue eyes like drowned periwinkles. He drank from the moment he woke up to the moment he went to sleep and was never entirely sober. He assured anyone who asked that he played better that way, and certainly he was an excellent musician – despite, or, if you believed him, because of his drinking habits. Unless you knew him, he was never visibly drunk – it was just that the higher his alcohol level, the more stately his deportment and his speech became. Annie liked him very much – there was a basic kindness and honesty about him that she admired.

'What did you want, anyway?' Annie asked. 'Anything I can do for you?'

'Safety pin,' he said, searching for and failing to find any longer way of saying it. 'The hook on my cummerbund seems to have yielded to overwhelming forces. Perhaps in your magic bag –?'

'Of course – a little thing like that's nothing to me,' Annie said, reaching for her big leather shoulder-bag, in which she had begun to keep a small general store of things for which she received requests – anything from sticking plasters and aspirins to rosin, A-strings and score-markers. In the beginning needy players would wander about the backstage area calling vaguely 'Has anybody got –', but now they came straight to Annie, and she found this automatic assumption that she could provide rather pleasant and flattering. It even now extended to non-material things, such as how to spell *parallel*, and where did you get the train for Chichester from.

'Here we are,' she said, emerging with the required safety pin, and catching the helpless look in Angus's eye she said resignedly, 'Do you want me to pin it for you?'

'Please,' he said, handing her the strip of black, pleated satin and revolving to present his back to her. 'Such a timely ministration –' he murmured happily. Annie eyed the crumpled material with distaste and stretched to place it around his barrel-shaped body where his trousers met his shirt.

'Could do with a wash,' she muttered, and heaved the ends together. 'No wonder it broke,' she said. 'Are you sure it's yours?'

'I fear the equatorial dimensions – rapid expansion – excess of nourishment of the liquid sort –' he burbled on happily while Annie achieved the impossible and married the two ends of the cummerbund with the presiding pin. 'So nice to have your arms round me,' he said suddenly and quite plainly. 'Perhaps my only chance.'

' 'Ere 'ere 'ere, wot's goin' on?' a cheerful shout assailed them. 'Get your hands off this man, I tell you, he's spoken for!' It was Ted Willment, principal trumpet and Angus's closest friend.

'Hello, Ted, did you want something too?' Annie greeted him.

'Only what we all want, precious – a squint down your cleavage to set us up for the fray tonight,' Ted said cheerfully. He stepped behind her and passed his arms round her to grasp Angus's waist beyond her. 'Come on, Annie,

20

give us a squeeze,' he clowned. It was unfortunate that at that moment of – fairly – innocent horseplay, Ivor Hotchkiss came along. He stopped abruptly and stared down his perfect Grecian nose at them, his blue eyes frosty, no hair of his golden curly crop out of place.

'Do you think this kind of behaviour is entirely approp-riate?' he asked with icy contempt. 'Can't you restrain your animal spirits until you are in the privacy of your own rooms?'

'Oh piss off, Ivor,' Ted said pleasantly. 'You're only jealous because you can't have a go.'

'I have no wish to "have a go" as you put it,' he went on coldly. 'I said all along it was a mistake to have a woman in this position, but when that woman has, apparently, the morals of an alley-cat, it is doubly a mistake.'

Ted felt Annie brace with anger at the remark, and to forestall her he said mockingly, 'I've always wondered what sort of a kiss a Hotchkiss is. Show us how you do it, Ivor.' He moved to one side of Annie, and said pleasantly to Angus, 'Do you know what Ivor's middle initials stand for – V.L.?'

'Tell me, tell me,' Angus said, catching on to the line.

'Very Large. Ivor Very Large Hotchkiss.'

Ivor's ivory cheeks grew two round red patches, but he feigned to ignore the sniggering duo, and instead looked Annie offensively up and down and said, 'And another thing – your clothes are entirely unsuitable for your job. Tony at least had the decency to dress properly when on duty.'

'Tony wore a dinner-jacket. I'm wearing a cocktail dress, which is the feminine equivalent,' Annie pointed out, keeping her temper.

'And how!' Ted murmured. Annie's black cocktail frock had a low front, no sleeves, and very little back at all. She thought it was very fetching.

'It's a dress designed to draw attention to yourself, arouse men's lust,' Ivor said. 'You might consider the effect it will have on the evening's performance before you arrive dressed like that. Or perhaps you don't care about the music?'

'Now look,' Annie said hotly, 'if you consider a musician –

21

a *real* musician – could be put off by the sight of a little perfectly decent bare flesh, then you should be out front vetting the audience as well. You're talking absolute nonsense, and you know it.'

'It isn't nonsense at all. Suitable clothing is a requirement of any job which places you in the public eye –'

'I'll come to work bloody topless if it suits me, without asking *your* permission,' Annie said, losing her temper abruptly. She was immediately sorry – it was her business to get on with the orchestra members – but then Ivor obviously had it in for her. At this point Angus took up her cause.

'Look here, Ivor,' he said, 'you aren't on the Board yet, you know.'

'I soon will be,' he said, turning suddenly and savagely on him. 'And when I am, I'll remember *your* name, my friend, don't you worry.'

There was a brief silence of shock at the naked malice exposed, and then Ted, who alone had kept cool, said, 'Oh, wrap it up, Ivor, your wee moustache is showing. Why don't you go and do something useful, like writing *Mein Kampf*, instead of coming round bullying us poor workers? I think Annie's dress is very nice, and no one but you has complained. Even Percy thought she looked pretty, so that shows you. Oh, and by the way, Annie, I wondered if I could have a borrow of your lipsalve, if you've got it in your magic bag?'

He turned a deliberate shoulder on Ivor, giving Annie the chance to rearrange her face while delving into her bag for the salve, and Ivor, perhaps realising he was bested, stalked away without another word. Angus watched him anxiously.

'He really meant it, you know,' he said when Ivor had gone.

'Oh balls,' Ted said easily. 'He's just a nut-case. He likes throwing his weight around.'

'What makes him such an amazing prig?' Annie asked.

'Did you say prig or prick?'

'Yes.'

Ted laughed. 'I don't know. I used to think he was queer, but it isn't that. He has a stupendously beautiful girl-friend. He's in the next room to mine at the hotel, and I can hear them at it through the wall: his grunts interspersed with "Is that comfortable for you, dear?" '

'I don't believe you,' Annie laughed.

'Well, I don't guarantee the exact words.'

'Still, he seems to have it in for me for some reason,' Annie said sadly.

'I think perhaps he resents your popularity,' Angus said unexpectedly. 'He is a handsome man, and yet you and other women show little interest in him. I imagine no one ever loved him very much, not even his mother, and so he craves power as a substitute for love.'

'Cor, listen to that,' Ted said, gaping with amazement at Angus. 'I never knew you done psychology as well as Hegelian neo-positivism, old cock.'

Angus ignored him. 'The difficulty is that it's now too late to compensate. A power-drive like his can be very dangerous.'

'Don't worry, Angus sweetheart,' Ted said largely, flinging an arm round Angus's broad shoulders. 'I'll protect you.'

Annie had looked at her watch. 'My God,' she exclaimed, 'look at the time! Get lined up, lads – it's time. I must go and round up my other stray sheep.'

'Coom by, Shep, coom by!' Ted called after her, adding a few sharp sheep-trial whistles as she sped away, laughing, to chase up the rest of the orchestra.

By the time they were all waiting in the wings for their entrance, the amazing grape-vine had spread the word of the disagreement with Ivor Hotchkiss, and Doris Walker took Annie to one side to say, 'Keep clear of that Ivor, dear, he's a bad lot. He's got a lot of influence in high places, and he can make trouble for people he doesn't like.'

'It was all so silly,' Annie told her. 'Trying to put on that my dress was indecent.'

'It's very nice, dear, and it suits you. When you've got a nice body, it's only natural to want to show it off. But Ivor's

23

got one or two of the older chaps on his side, and it would be simpler all round if you wore something with sleeves another time.'

'Wouldn't that look like giving in?' Annie asked, angered and embarrassed by the whole idea. Doris nodded her massive coiffure wisely.

'There are times, dear, when giving in is the best way of winning. There's pride and pride, you know. Men aren't very bright, poor creatures, and it's sometimes best to humour them – I'm all for an easy life.' And she left it at that to take her place on the rapidly-filling platform. Last on, as usual, were Ted and Angus, Angus because he had been finishing a last Scotch, Ted because he had been talking somewhere to someone. Annie did a rapid count, and then went to tell the conductor and leader that they were ready.

The leader took his place, the conductor came on, the applause died away, and the music began. Annie paused for a while in the curtained entrance to watch and listen, to view the whole which was the end result of so much work, her own small contribution included. Such a different aspect the orchestra presented to the public from that to be seen at rehearsals! The men in white tie and tails, the women in long black evening-gowns, at first sight their individuality was submerged in the uniform black-and-white formality. They were so different from the noisy, scruffy, cheerful group of the daytime. Now they sat grave and respectable, their faces set with concentration, their eyes fixed on the music, flicking now and then briefly to the conductor. Now they were the skilled artists, re-creating through their extraordinary talents the music that had once lived in the brain of a man long dead.

They played, and during the rest bars they remained motionless, their heads gravely bent as if listening to the music; now they were dedicated musicians, submerged in the wholeness of the music. But, with only the slightest shift of focus, Annie could see them all in another light: the microscope of her knowledge of them could see that the immaculate black-and-white evening-dress was in fact often

24

a draggled and despised uniform, grease-spotted, creased, and stained; the grave concentration and the dreamy, faraway look often concealed pedestrian thoughts as to what colour to redecorate the sitting-room and whether the car would get through its MOT next week.

And with another shift of focus, they were every orchestra she had ever listened to. The timpanist, for instance, sitting very erect at the back within his magic circle of kettle-drums – his evening-suit *was* immaculate, one of the few whose shoulders were not sprinkled with dandruff and loose hairs; his shoes shone like glass, no hair on his neat head was out of place, and his neatly manicured hands had about them a good deal of plain, tasteful gold jewellery. All timpanists were neat and precise and rather elegant like that – or so it seemed. Just as second violins were saddened, if not embittered, by perpetually playing a background to the first violins, who had all the fun; and woodwind players were refined and well mannered and frequently even aristocratic; and double-bass players were very jolly and hearty and kind; and trumpet players were given to salty wit and pints of ale.

And horn players? she asked herself abruptly, catching herself out in the act of bringing the mental subject round to them. What have you got to conclude about horn players? That they are charming, self-confident, ambitious and cold? Perhaps. Perhaps. Ivor Hotchkiss might be an extreme form of them. Geoffrey Hamilton was possibly typical. It was no good telling herself bad things about Geoffrey. There was nothing bad about him that she didn't know, and had always known, but it didn't make any difference. She had loved him, and did love him still, and perhaps some of her contentment in this job had been due to the feeling of being back in the swim, and yet safe from him.

And that, she told herself, is enough of that. There was nothing to be gained from thinking about Geoffrey but restless nights. The overture was almost finished, it was time she went to alert the soloist, who would be coming on for the next piece. She took another look back at the once-again-whole orchestra, a single black-and-white body with eighty

25

heads, and at the audience, quiet, concentrating, wrapped in the music that was being drawn for them out of small black marks on white paper, and wondered if she would ever again be able to listen to a concert with the undivided attention of a plain-and-simple music-lover. She thought not. But there was no way back – there was never any way back.

The party was given in another hall, which had been decorated for the occasion by the civic authorities, who were also providing the food and drink, with what appeared to be bunting kept over from the Coronation, so faded and rain-marked and generally moth-eaten was it. Annie thought the hall could have done without it, having apparently been recently redecorated in a very fetching shade of eau-de-Nil picked out with white, but perhaps they had wanted to show willing.

The crowd which filled the hall looked very distinguished, for those members of the orchestra who had come – which was nearly all of them – had come in their evening-clothes, with the exception of Warren Stacker, who had changed his tails for a white dinner-jacket and his white tie for a claret-coloured velvet bow, and Doris Walker, who had refused to come in what she called, with cheerful irreverence, her 'overalls'.

'I wear that damned black rag every concert, I simply can't be jolly in it,' she said. She had changed into a wide, floating chiffon creation in a violent pea-green shade that completely disregarded her anatomy. She looked vast and uncontrolled in it, like a runaway cauldron of soup, topped by her extraordinary orange hair that under the fluorescent lighting turned a shade no organic material ever was.

She made a welcome splash of colour, though, along with the few female guests from outside the orchestra, one of whom was, of course, Julie. Annie felt quite proud to be with her, for she looked elegant and pretty and very proper in a clinging blue silk that was just the right shade for her colouring.

26

'Frightful though the end result may be,' Annie said to her when she managed at last to locate Julie and Pat in the crowd, 'I agree with Doris about the black rags. When you wear that sort of thing to work in, you can't help wanting a bit of a change for pleasure wear.'

'Mm,' Julie agreed with reservations. 'But black does happen to suit you marvellously well, with your white skin and blonde hair. I can't help thinking a colour would diminish you.'

'I'm already in trouble over this dress,' Annie said, and told them the story of Ivor Hotchkiss's objections.

'Which one is he?' Pat asked. 'I simply must see this man who can object to a sight of a beautiful woman's body. He must be a biological rarity all right.'

'That's him over there, with the willowy lady in lilac,' Annie said, pointing discreetly. 'I must say, she does seem to be fairly well covered up, except for her arms.'

'She has nothing to *un*cover,' Pat said scornfully. 'Straight up and down like a Boy Scout's tent. I don't entirely trust men who choose women for themselves that are the same shape as boys. It seems to be a social sickness. Now, I like women that you can tell in the dark are women,' he went on, edging nearer to Annie.

'Watch it,' she said, 'Julie's looking.'

'Don't mind me,' Julie said unconcernedly. 'I don't mind you taking the edge off him for me.'

'Julie!' Annie cried, opening her eyes wide. Pat grinned delightedly.

'Coming out of her shell these days, isn't she?' he said. Julie looked at him with withering scorn.

'That's the trouble with you men, you can't see what's under your own noses. You're easy enough to fool.' Pat gave her a hug, and she smiled up at him with perfect accord.

'Ah, there you are at last,' Ted cried, bursting through the nearest dam of bodies at that moment. He was carrying a glass of whisky in each hand, and his white tie had been thrust into his trouser pocket, from which it was coyly peeping like a white mouse trying to escape. 'I've been

27

looking for you everywhere. I got you whisky – I suppose that's what you drink.' He said it as if it was the only thing anyone would drink, if they had any sense.

'Hello,' Annie said, and realised that introductions were necessary. 'Pat and Julie, this is Ted Willment, first trumpet. My sister and brother-in-law, Julie and Patrick Tarrent.'

They shook hands all round, Annie having first relieved Ted of one of the glasses.

'Did you enjoy the concert?' Ted asked. It was the polite question that musicians always ask of outsiders; and just as children always answer 'How do you do?' with 'Very well, thank you', so concert-goers always answer the rhetorical question literally.

'Very much, thank you,' Julie said politely, meaning as little by her answer as Ted had by the question. Pat got down immediately to more personal things.

'I thought you played very well,' he said. 'Wonderfully crisp and attacking.'

'You mean me personally?' Ted asked, rather blankly. Pat nodded.

'Of course. It isn't often that phrase at the end of the first movement can be heard properly, though I suppose that's partly the conductor's fault.'

'Do you play?' was the inevitable next question.

'I used to play for fun until a few years back,' Pat said, 'but a slight car accident put me out of the running.' He made a casual gesture towards his mouth, to the unnoticeable scar on the lip that had spoiled his *embouchure*. Ted nodded gravely.

'Bad luck,' he said with gruff understatement. Julie and Annie exchanged an amused glance. Manly sympathy was expressed that way, it said.

'I suppose your lip is insured?' Annie said, more than half-joking. Ted looked embarrassed.

'Well –' he began, almost shuffling his feet. Annie grinned delightedly.

'Really? How much for? Oh do tell!' He refused. She urged. 'Come on, tell!'

'Look here, can't you keep your sister in order?' Ted appealed to Julie and Pat together.

'No. Never could,' Julie said, smiling at her affectionately.

'I *could*,' Pat said, 'but my wife wouldn't let me.' He and Ted looked at each other with approval. That mysterious rapport that exists between males had been born out of those few unimportant exchanges. 'Look, if you aren't doing anything, would you like to join us for a bite of supper? We were going to drag Annie away as soon as she could decently absent herself.'

'I'd love to, if –' Ted looked from one of the women to the other, his eyes lingering on Annie.

'Do join us,' Annie said cordially, and Julie nodded her agreement. Annie was perfectly aware of what Pat was up to, and that Julie was going along with Pat for the sake of peace. It seemed a strange reversal of tactics for Pat to want to pair her off with a musician, but she liked Ted and had no objection to making a fourth with him at the dinner table. Anything more than that – the thought made her study Ted rather more closely than she had before. He was of middle height, nice figure, pleasant, almost handsome face; brass-players' broad back and strong, short hands; brass-players' long, firm, narrow-lipped mouth. She gave a sudden shudder. She had never noticed his mouth before. Feeling her gaze, or perhaps her shudder, he turned his head abruptly and their eyes met. Good God, she thought, what's come over me? She found herself suddenly in her imagination running her fingers through that straight, silky, toffee-brown hair that fell forward over his forehead giving him a spurious look of innocence. She banished the thought hastily, and without thinking quickly swallowed the drink in her glass in order to be able to say, shall we go?

She didn't get a single word of it out. The neat spirit, which she had forgotten was whisky, hit the back of her throat and she gasped, which made her in turn start to cough, and seconds later she was in the clutches of a paroxysm as the spirit went everywhere, including into her lungs.

29

'Careful!' Pat remonstrated. 'You're throwing it around like Tizer!'

'Are you all right?' Julie asked as Pat held Annie's shoulder with one hand and gave her a few brotherly thumps on the back with the other, which caused her to gasp even more. Ted produced a handkerchief from his pocket and offered it to her to mop herself with.

'Here,' he said. 'It isn't spotless, but it's only been used foɪ polishing my horn, not for blowing on or anything. I'm sorry the drink got you. I thought you were used to whisky.' Since Annie was still incapable of speech, though she was recovering, he asked Pat anxiously, 'Does she drink?'

'Oh yes,' Pat said drily. 'She drinks all right. I think you just caught her unawares.'

And what does he mean by that? Annie wondered as they walked out from the hall a few minutes later into the cool fresh night. For a man, Pat was sometimes uncomfortably discerning.


They dined at a very posh restaurant built out on a jetty over the sea, a few miles up the coast. It was famous for its fish dishes, and was *the* elegant place to go for the members of Swansea's high society. Ted was slightly cross and Annie not at all surprised to see four other members of the orchestra dining there, each alone with a paramour. They all pretended not to see Ted and Annie as they came in, and were very glad when Ted and Annie were placed at a good distance away, at a table by a window that looked down a small steep drop to the sea.

The lighting was low and pink – very flattering to all ages – and the tables candle-lit, and, outside, a moon in the dark sky was beating a path of silver over the quiet water.

'Tremendously romantic,' Pat commented as they sat down. 'Seems almost a waste for us. We ought to be two pairs of lovers. Never mind – it's amazing what a couple of glasses of champagne can do.'

30

'What are we celebrating?' Julie asked him. He winked at her across the table.

'I'll tell you later,' he said.

# THREE

They started off with crayfish bisque, and to go with it Pat ordered a very delicate, very dry champagne. Baskets of delicious home-made wholemeal bread were placed on the table, and the nutty, wheaten flavour was the perfect foil to the exotic soup. The conversation quickly grew animated, and the four of them seemed to get along with no trouble, as if they had known each other for years, which was odd since a lot of the time they were asking questions about each other.

They discovered, for instance, that Ted was one of the few top British brass players who had come up through a university rather than through works or military bands. 'No other country can come near our brass, because of that brass-band tradition,' he said. 'I found the difference enormous, my first teacher being an ex-Black Dyke man, and my second a professor from an American university. Still it did give me an all-round experience.'

His all-round experience seemed to have made him good company at least, Annie thought, for he had a lively mind, was well informed, and could talk on many subjects. His interests seemed varied, and some of them at least coincided with her own. Riding, for one – horses had always been a passion with Annie, right from childhood.

'I love riding too,' Ted said when this came up in the conversation. 'I don't get much chance now of course – we seem to work all the hours God sends, and a few over – but whenever I can get away, there's this place I know in the Brecon Beacons – not all that far from here, really. It's about fifteen miles from Abergavenny, a tiny little village in the heart of the hills, and I stay there with this marvellous woman who cooks exactly like heaven, and I ride out every day, right over the mountains.'

'It sounds fabulous!' Annie said eagerly, imagining it.

'And then home after a long day in the saddle, and a hot

bath, a wonderful meal, and then an evening by a great roaring log fire swapping anecdotes with Diana.' Annie looked at his expression, and found herself, absurdly, wondering how much this Diana meant to him. Why on earth should she care? But all the same, dreams when spoken aloud had no right to come ready-peopled.

'You must come there with me some time – you'd love it,' Ted said.

'Yes, I'd love to,' Annie replied, but it sounded only polite, and he quickly changed the subject to cars, on which both he and Pat had a lot to say, recounting stories of dreadful experiences with cars that fell to pieces in the same moment that they fell off the production line. Julie joined in with stories about dreadful drivers, and this kept them occupied until the second course arrived. Julie, who could never get enough shellfish, had chosen langoustines; Ted and Pat were having the restaurant's speciality, which was bass with dill, each fish cooked individually in foil in its own juices and served with plain boiled new potatoes and lots of butter; and Annie had chosen rather plainer fare, sole poached in butter. A huge bowl of excellent green salad was brought for them all to help themselves, and the wine waiter shimmered into view at Pat's elbow.

'What shall we drink? Shall we stick with champagne, or shall we have something different?' Everyone looked politely at everyone else, not wanting to make the decision, and finally Pat turned towards Annie. 'Come on, Annie, you're the one with the strong character. Tell us what we should drink.'

'What I'd really like, if they have one here,' she said at length, 'is a very good Muscadet.'

'Good choice,' Pat applauded her, and turned to the wine waiter.

'We have a rather fine 1976, sir,' he suggested, and this was approved, and brought, and the conversation returned to cars and the self-acclamatory subject of who were the world's worst drivers, a subject on which every car driver that ever was has plenty to say, and plenty of examples to back up his opinion. 'I remember one time when I was going over the Brenner Pass –' and 'When I was in Los Angeles last –' and 'If you've ever driven the coast road from Monte –' and even 'You've only got to drive along the Uxbridge Road from Acton to Southall –' fluttered about the table like moths attracted to the flame of self-esteem. If Annabel said rather less than the other three, it wasn't because she had fewer thoughts on the subject, but because she didn't know who it was who was pressing her foot under the table, or whether it was intentional, and there are few more absorbing puzzles than that in a woman's experience.

The conversation drifted on. 'It's a curious thing about fish,' Ted said, 'how no one ever takes the fish's part. Almost anything else that's killed or chased or hunted or captured or eaten has someone, often many people, to champion it. But the fish? Who cares for fish?'

'*I* do. Yum yum,' Julie interpolated. Ted let this pass.

'I mean, look at the fuss that's made over fox-hunting and hare-coursing, and even over shooting brainless inbred game-birds. But no one ever marches about with placards depicting the trout's last lonely agony.'

'You're making me feel horribly guilty about this sole,' Annie said, looking directly at him in an endeavour to read his foot in his eye. She learnt nothing.

'You should, if you have a soul,' he said. Pat groaned.

'No fish puns, please – Julie and Annie have a million of them, and once started they're virtually unstoppable.'

Annie now had to justify her earnest gaze. Off the top of her head she said, 'You're right about the fish, though. Why –' inspiration – 'even vegetarians sometimes make exceptions to the flesh-rule over fish. Poor little blighters.'

'They remain the only wild creature that's hunted for food for ordinary people,' Ted finished. There was a short silence.

'Not much you can say after that, is there?' Pat said, and after exchanging a slightly puzzled look, they all started to laugh. 'What a conversation-stopper!' Pat said afterwards. 'Well, does anyone want a dessert, or shall we go on to coffee?'

35

'Of course I do,' Julie said indignantly. 'It's amazing how you men pretend to despise afters when you're eating in a restaurant. At home you get through two or three helpings of pudding, even on a weekday.'

'Is nothing sacred?' Pat groaned, putting his face in his hands. 'Now you know why I'm the shape I am.'

'I thought that was rugger,' Annie said innocently, and he reached out and tweaked her nose.

'No cheek from you, infant,' he said, and Annie saw Ted looking from one to the other of them, as if trying to judge the exact relationship between them. The waiter brought the menus again, and after a brief consideration Julie and Annie chose Chartreuse ice-cream, Pat chose *fraises des bois*, and Ted the blackberry and melon salad.

'Aren't they manly,' Julie jeered. 'Only fresh fruit for dessert, like American society hostesses!'

'You're amazingly uppity tonight, my girl,' Pat said to her threateningly. 'You wait till I get you home.'

'What about me?' Annie said incautiously. 'I'm uppity too – am I going to get away with it?'

'No – Ted'll take care of you,' Pat retorted quickly. Oh well, Annie thought, I asked for it. Annoyingly, the footsy nudge that accompanied the words could equally well have come from either of them; but at least she now knew, if nothing else, that it was intentional.

It was late when, pleasantly full and in accord with one another, they walked out into the salt-scented night, and shivered a little at the contrasting chill of the air. They lingered for a few minutes in the car park, not wanting the pleasant evening to end, until Pat finally exerted himself to say, 'Well, we'd better be getting back to our hotel, I suppose. We may have to knock up the landlady to get in as it is. Where are you staying, Ted?'

'Out at the Osborne Hotel. That's one thing about this orchestra – they do at least get you decent dosses. Most of us are at the Osborne, and the others are at the Langton.'

'You're at the Osborne too, aren't you, Annie?' Julie asked.

'Oh yes,' Annie said. 'The admin staff are all in town except me. I'm supposed to stick with the players through thick and thin, bailing them out of whatever trouble they get themselves in when they're off the platform. It has its advantages – they can't give me materially worse quarters than the musicians.'

'So will you go back with Ted in his car, then?' Pat asked, sticking to the point, which Annie had subconsciously been avoiding. Ted answered for her, with a naturalness that almost shamed her.

'Oh yes, of course I'll drive Annie back. Well, thanks very much for a lovely evening. I hope we'll meet again some time.'

'We'll probably drop in on our way out of town tomorrow,' Pat said. 'Good night, then.'

'Goodnight, Annie – sleep tight,' Julie added.

'Fraid not – I'll have sobered up by the time I get to bed,' she joked in reply, and with last lingering waves the couples separated and drove off in opposite directions, one car towards the town and the other towards Langland Bay.

'They're nice, your brother and sister,' Ted said after a while. Annie was staring out of the side window at the moonlit waters and wondering what was going to happen next.

'Yes. Julie and I have always been very close.'

'I could see that. And Pat – he's a good sort of bloke, isn't he?' There was a faint question in what ought to have been a statement.

'Mm,' Annie said, and then, because this sounded ungracious, 'He's a good friend.'

This seemed to satisfy Ted, and they drove in silence until they reached the bay. Then, instead of turning into the hotel drive, Ted turned the car towards the headland, and stopped there where the trees broke and there was a view. Oho, Annabel thought. The engine was turned off, and in the darkness she could hear his heavy breathing. It gave her an insane desire to giggle. It was all so *déjà-vu*, so very much the sort of thing that happened to one when one was a teenager.

37

And yet, where else did most things start in this day and age but in a car? She waited for the casual, clumsy, inevitable next move.

'Want to walk fot a bit?' he asked her abruptly. 'I feel a bit stuffed up with all that food.'

Surprised, she lost her tongue for a moment, and then agreed quickly, to cover up. He got out of the car and came round to let her out, and they walked in silence along the crest with the sea below them, crawling black upon silver. The slightest, lightest touch upon her arm. 'You're cold. You'd better have my jacket. There really isn't very much of that dress, is there?'

If there was one thing in the world Annie hated, it was having a man's jacket draped over her shoulders – she would always rather be cold than look a fool. But she was slightly unnerved by this remote-control approach, and so she suffered him to drape her in silence, and they walked on until he judged it was enough, and turned back towards the car. Annabel was now thoroughly confused. It must have been Pat in the restaurant, then. Ted – she didn't even know if he was married. She had thought not. Had she been conceited to assume he would make a pass at her? Obviously so. Take a hundred lines – I must not anticipate the grab. In the car again she took the first opportunity, gratefully, to shrug off his jacket, and became aware, quite abruptly, that he smelled quite delicious – a very faint fragrance, quite unlike the usual run-of-the-mill bang-on-the-head type of commercial after-shaves, mixed with the warm biscuity smell of his own self.

The drive to the hotel was very brief, and as soon as the car stopped she jumped out and waited while he locked it, impatient to get inside and end this irritatingly ambiguous situation. He seemed to take for ever, collecting his discarded tail-coat from where she had so churlishly dropped it, sorting out some papers, and finally emerging with his trumpet-case in one hand while he locked the car door with the other.

'Do you take that with you to your room?' she asked, interested. He glanced down and shrugged.

38

'I'm never parted from it. I don't feel easy leaving it anywhere. I couldn't replace it.'

'Is it so valuable?'

'Not in terms of money, but it's unique. Every trumpet has its own tone, and this is the one I'm used to. I couldn't play another.' Still he didn't move, and Annie made a movement towards the hotel, cold again and growing more irritable.

'Shall we go in?' she said.

'Annie –' he said, and she was forced to turn back and look at him. His straight, autumn-coloured hair fell between his eyes like the forelock of a pony. He was staring at her with a slightly troubled look, as though he were working out a particularly difficult sum in mental arithmetic. What on earth is he going to ask me? she wondered. Lend us a quid, or will you please not wear that dress to work any more?

'I want you really most dreadfully. Would you like to come to bed with me?'

A pang, like the sudden awareness of hunger. She licked her lips nervously. Various considerations to do with her job and the wisdom of the move fleeted through her brain, and were instantly dismissed. What the hell, she thought. No one's paying me for my chastity.

'Yes,' she said. 'I think I would.'

A weight seemed to lift visibly from his shoulders. He grew an inch in height, and came forward with confidence to take her hand with his free one and led her towards the side door of the hotel as if he had been doing this all his life.

Which, she thought as they passed through the dimly lit foyer and up the stairs, considering his line of work, he probably had.


She was stunned, exalted, breathless, ravished, amazed, even a little shocked. What made one man a better lover than another? She had always believed it was in the mind – that if you were in love with someone, they were automatically more exciting than someone else. Yet here she was, not at all in love with Ted, only liking him rather a lot, and lying dazed

39

and staggered in his bed beside his flat-out, sweating body, wondering where she had been all her life and what life had been for until that moment.

She turned her head carefully to look at him. He was lying on his front beside her, his head turned away. The shape of his skull was good, a curve you wanted to put your hand round, his neck strong, his shoulders wide, white-skinned and gold-dusted with freckles, like the throat of an orchid. Backs, she thought, are fascinating, like the outsides of great buildings. Fronts have more detail, fan-vaulting and carved panelling, but backs are monumental.

With an economical movement he turned his head on the pillow. His face was too close to hers for her to be able to judge what his expression was. He had the most extraordinarily dark brown eyes, richly dark, unlike anything else that was brown in the world. One could say of blue eyes that they were like cornflowers or summer skies, but brown eyes were like nothing but brown eyes.

'I never knew a man with brown eyes before,' she said.

'Did you think they were the province of females, then?'

'Why are you called Ted? It doesn't suit you at all.'

'Because my name, Edward Willment, is unpronounceable. I share that distinction with Edward Woodward – he's called Ted too. I don't know what my parents were thinking of. Well, I do – my brothers are called Albert and David. My father liked the names of Princes of Wales. It could have been worse – we might have ended up as Christian and Louis.'

'Tell me about yourself.'

'There's nothing to tell. I'm as ordinary as anyone can be.'

'Not ordinary. You have brown eyes.'

He stretched the additional required half inch and kissed her lips, lightly as if tasting them the way one would sniff a rose.

'Tell me about your parents, your home and so on,' she demanded again.

'I was born in Oxfordshire,' he said. 'My father is a skilled labourer. He works in a car factory, putting seat-belts on

40

middle-priced saloons. My mother is an invoice typist in a clothing factory. I have two brothers and two sisters.'

'Are any of them married?'

'All of them, except me. And they all have children. We're an ordinary, fertile family.'

'Go on.'

'I went to the local grammar school, and then to university.'

'Oxford?'

'Reading.'

'Where you studied the trumpet.'

'Not straight away. My father played the trombone in the car-works band, and he encouraged me to play. I learned trombone at school, but he wanted me to play the French horn. He said that was the aristocrat of the brass family. So I went to Reading and played the French horn.'

'Then how did you get to the trumpet?'

He hitched himself up on to one elbow as if this was going to be a long tale and so he needed to be comfortable. She turned on to her side and stroked his leg absently as he spoke.

'It's a bit of a story,' he said. 'I went to London one summer to work during the vacation, and I got myself a place to stay, a bedsitter in a big house in Earl's Court. Living in the same house was this crazy lady.'

'*Cherchez la femme*,' Annie murmured. He did not seem to hear.

'She was living in one tiny room. She was a writer, and a marvellous person, and tremendously sexy. It seemed to ooze out of her pores. I was – you might not believe this – still a virgin. My family were rather old-fashioned and strict about things like that, and somehow, even though I was at university, I'd never really got round to it.'

'Getting round isn't the way I'd describe it – but go on.'

'Well, I fell madly in love with her. And in the course of being in bed with her I told her I was studying the French horn. She was shocked. "That blasted braying tin whistle?" she said. She was mad about trumpets – always had been – and now at the age of thirty-six – nearly twice my age, you

41

see? – she was taking lessons, learning to play it. She'd always wanted to, you see. She was taking lessons from Bob Akroyd – do you know him? He's the principal trumpet with the English Sinfonietta.'

'Yes,' Annie said abruptly. The English Sinfonietta was Geoffrey's orchestra. She knew many of the players. Ted's face was innocent, or she would have wondered how much was intended by the question.

'Well, she converted me,' he went on. 'She taught me everything I know about making love, so I had to go along with her, to be polite. She took me to one of her lessons, and I listened to Bob Akroyd playing, and I was converted. The French horn was nothing to the trumpet. So I transferred to the Royal Academy, and when I came out of there I went to the Youth Orchestra for two years, and then came here as co-principal.'

'That was quick work. You must have had talent to get to the top so quickly.'

'I think I had a natural feeling for it,' he said.

'As you have for other things,' she murmured, still stroking his leg. He smiled, pleased.

'Do you think so?'

'Don't be too modest. This thirty-six-year-old of yours was evidently working on malleable clay.' He put his arms round her, and she took his face in her hands and held it still, and ran the tip of her tongue around the limit of his mouth. 'Your mouth fascinates me. You have hardly any top lip at all – just a little pink point in the middle – *here* – where your mouthpiece presses. And when you kiss it's as if you have extra muscles that other people don't have.' Still holding his head, she kissed him as if she were the man, and he remained motionless while she did, as if he were afraid he would break if he made any sudden movement.

'I seem to have a lot to thank her for,' Annie said at last, releasing him. Ted took a long, shaky breath.

'Don't think it's anything but way in the past. What I have for you is for you. Look – do you think I could be like this again so soon for a memory?'

42

'No. I didn't mean that. I only meant she taught you well.'

Then she was in his arms, and he was sliding over on top of her again, mouth to mouth and breast to breast and arms wrapped around each other tightly as if they were afraid someone was going to come and drag them apart any moment. This time it seemed all over in a flash, and they both fell instantly asleep, tumbled together heedlessly like puppies, and slept until the chillier air of dawn half-woke them and they crawled under the covers and cuddled together and slept again.

# FOUR

The first moment of the first time you wake beside someone new is very important. In the heat of the moment, or moments, the night before, anything goes, but in the cold light of morning, especially if you have eaten or drunk too much the night before, the person you found enchanting in the dark can turn your stomach. Annie, awakening suddenly with a sense of having forgotten something or missed something, slowly became aware that she was not in her own bed, slowly remembered what had happened, and reached out cautiously to encounter the sleeping hump of the man in the bed beside her.

Very slowly she turned her head. He was hunched up, curled round like a hamster, and his tobacco-blonde hair was something of the colour of a hamster's coat too. It fell straight and silken, hardly ruffled at all, across his forehead. Beneath it he slept determinedly. In repose his face looked younger. Even awake he had an innocent look, but asleep he looked absurdly young, too young to have been doing what he had been doing. But all right. Quite all right. He didn't make her feel awful. Only affectionate. He was still as charming as he had been last night.

That settled, she looked at her watch, which she hadn't taken off the night before. Still early – no panic. Time for a bath, and then breakfast. A huge breakfast. It was strange, but she had had an enormous dinner which ought to have lasted her a week, and yet she was absolutely starving, far more hungry than she usually was when she woke. Absolutely *ravishing* as Julie sometimes said.

She jumped up, thoroughly grateful that Ted's room had a bathroom *en suite*, for she did not think she could face putting on her clothes to walk down a corridor to a bathroom. The sound of the water running must have woken him, for when she came back into the room he was sitting up,

45

stretching and yawning like someone in a play showing that they had just woken up.

'What a lovely sound that is first thing in the morning,' he said. 'Hello. Kiss.'

She sat down on his side of the bed and kissed him, lightly on the lips. He scrutinised her carefully.

'What?' she asked, nervously.

'How are you feeling? No regrets? No guilt?'

'Should I have? You aren't married.'

'That's true,' he said. 'Is that all?'

'How do you expect me to feel?'

'I hope you feel rested and invigorated and ready to face a new day with a clear mind and a sound digestion.'

She laughed. 'I'm starving.'

'A good healthy reaction. And how nice to hear you laugh. I'm glad you aren't one of those people who wake up in a bad temper and can't be talked to until after eleven.'

'*You* evidently aren't,' she said, sidestepping the apparent assumption that he was going to experience a lot of her early morning moods. 'I'm having a bath, and then I must go and get some clean clothes, and then I'm going to get a simply huge breakfast.'

'Good thinking. I shall join in with the programme with the greatest of pleasure. Leave your bathwater for me. I don't suppose you're very dirty – and I have a feeling that there might not be enough for two whole baths.'

She was a quick bather, in and out in five minutes. She scrambled with distaste into yesterday's clothes – why is it that the same-clothes-again feel so *scummy* when you haven't slept in your own bed? – and while Ted was still in the bath she called out, 'I'm off now – see you in the dining-room.'

'Hey!' he called. She returned from the door and poked her head into the bathroom.

'What?'

'Aren't you coming back here to call for me?'

'Better not,' she said, wishing he hadn't asked. She would have been glad not to spoil the mood. 'I don't think we had better go down together. We mustn't be obvious.'

46

'Mustn't we?' he seemed genuinely puzzled.

'It's better for the job if people didn't know how friendly we were.'

'They'll know,' he said flatly. 'You can't hide things like that.'

'As the actress said to the bishop. Look, they won't *know*. Let them guess all they like.'

He shrugged. 'As you please.'

'Don't be huffy,' she pleaded.

'I'm not. No, really I'm not. I only think it's effort wasted.'

'Okay,' she said, and went, circumspectly, to her own room.

She was almost the first in the dining-room: Ivor Hotchkiss was there, seated at a table with his bosom buddy, Glyn Paradine, the principal clarinet, and Annie gave them a polite wave before sitting on the other side of the room which she felt covered both politeness and common sense. The waiter came and she gave her order for a large breakfast – eggs, bacon, sausages, tomatoes, mushrooms and fried bread, to be followed with plenty of toast, and a pot of coffee. That, she felt, should stave off any ill-effects from over-exertion.

She was just feeling that she ought to have brought a paper to save her the embarrassment of being seen to be waiting for her food, when a car drew up outside and a moment later Angus came in. He ignored the other two men and made a bee-line for Annie. He looked to her as if he hadn't been to bed.

'You're up early,' she said cheerfully. 'Come and join me. Been for a swim or something?'

He shook his head, staring at her with his tragic eyes. 'Been to get this,' he said conspiratorially, drawing something out from his pocket below the level of the table-cloth. 'A laddie I know in the town – values friendship more than his license.'

'What is it?' Annabel couldn't actually see the object. With a glance over his shoulder, he drew it out and placed it on the table – a tiny bottle wrapped in brown paper.

'Fernet Branca,' he said. 'In the mornings, death seems a horrible reality. This stuff tastes like torture, but it holds things together.'

'Oh Angie,' Annie said, shaking her head sadly. 'Do you really feel that bad?'

He didn't answer her until with a furtive but evidently practised movement he had jerked the contents of the little bottle down his throat. 'I do now, but in five minutes I shall have returned to the land of the living.' He closed his eyes and composed his features as if in contemplation. Annie studied him. She supposed he ought to look ill, but in fact he looked just the same as he always did. His complexion was naturally pale, he never had any colour in his cheeks, and she had already decided that was a natural Glasgow pallor. His face was not unhandsome, firm-skinned, nice neat features, unexpectedly fine eyebrows, arched and dark and silky-haired, as if sketched in with the finest brush. His hair was dark with the slightest curl, and where the light caught it, it had a foxy-red glint that was attractive with his white skin.

He opened his eyes quite suddenly, and she was falling down into their fathomless depths.

'What do you think?' he asked her, as if at the end of some long peroration.

'You look fine,' she said. 'One wouldn't know if one didn't know.'

The waiter hovered near. 'Scrambled eggs and black coffee,' Angus said without looking at him. 'Amazing, the powers of recovery of the human frame, five minutes ago the words alone would have made me sick. You look wonderful this morning, blooming and lovely, my sunny-faced elf, as Rochester would say.'

'Rochester?'

*'Jane Eyre.'*

'Oh, of course – I was thinking of the limping cowboy. I always thought she treated him most ungraciously, refusing to wear the poor man's jewels. Continually taking him down a peg. Wanting to get married in her working clothes, that sort of thing.'

'And only really loving him when he was crippled,' Angus reminded her. 'But perhaps she was right. Undoubtedly he would have got bored with her if she had gone his way and become like all the others. And then, perhaps we really only love people when they're helpless, and only we can save them. There's a destructiveness about love, a perversity. Take Geoffrey Hamilton for instance – you know Geoffrey Hamilton?'

Annie felt herself going red, but she was saved the immediate necessity of answering by the advent of the waiter with Angus's eggs and a call to the telephone for her.

'I postponed your breakfast, madam, when I heard.'

'Thank you – excuse me, Angus.' As she got up she heard Angus behind her calling back the waiter in loud, insolent, Scottish tones.

'I ordered scrambled eggs, not grey plasticine. Look at them – rock hard. Scrambled eggs are supposed to be soft, golden yellow, moist, and hot. If your chef doesn't know how to make them, I shall be delighted to come into the kitchen and show him. Tak' them away, man, and tell him I'll have them made with eggs, butter, salt and pepper and *nothing else*. And if they're no' hot and moist when they reach me, you'll both have to start all over again.'

Smiling, Annie hurried out into the foyer where the desk clerk called her.

'Mrs Holst?' he asked, investing her with a status she didn't have. 'Here is your call.' It was the assistant concerts manager, who was staying in the town with the other non-playing staff, to say that the conductor had gone sick and that a last-minute replacement had been found.

'But he can't do the Bartok, he wants to do a Mozart instead, so there'll have to be an extra rehearsal this morning. Can you round up the necessary chaps before they scatter to the four winds? You know the form – the reduced orchestra. Two horns. No trumpets or trombones, of course.'

'Okay, will do,' she said resignedly. 'What's wrong with Rostrovitch, anyway?'

49

'Swansea Tummy, I think it's called. Get to it, kid.'

'Willco. See ya.'

'What's up?' Angus asked her as she returned to the table.

'No Sunday morning off for us, I'm afraid. Rossy's gone down with gyppy tummy, and they've got Arthur Standish to fill in, but he can't do the Bartok, so there's an extra rehearsal this morning for the Mozart he's doing instead.'

'Silly bugger,' Angus said contemptuously.

'Which?'

'Both of them.'

Out of the corner of her eye, Annie saw the other two men getting up to leave, and she jumped up quickly to catch them before they disappeared.

'Ivor, Glyn! Don't go – I have to speak to you.'

They came over without enthusiasm, and Annie told them the story. 'Sorry, but you're both going to be needed.'

'Okay,' Ivor said, shrugging, 'but what about *him*?' He nodded towards Angus. 'Is he going to be fit to play, after last night?'

Annie was so shocked at this coming out in the open that for a moment she had nothing to say, and Glyn chipped in nastily. 'Yes, I hope you're going to be able to manage, Angus. I don't like having to carry you all the time, to say nothing of –'

Angus jumped to his feet so violently that his chair fell over backwards, and Glyn flinched away as if he thought Angus was going to hit him. Angus's pale face was invested with two red patches, and his obvious anger was such that it would not have been surprising if he *had* taken a swing at his tormentor.

'You take that back, you bastard!' he shouted, his Glasgow accent very pronounced. 'You bloody well take that back, or I'll shove your teeth down your bloody Fascist throat. You just tell me here before witnesses when you've ever had to carry me. Carry me? You couldn't carry a lead part in a kids' pantomime, you no-balled little freak!'

'Angus, don't, please calm down. It doesn't help,' Annie begged him. She had seen Ivor's contented little smile at the

50

outburst. 'Glyn, I think you should take back what you said. It's a slander, and Angus has every right to be angry.'

'Quite the little Mary Poppins, aren't you?' Glyn sneered. 'As to slander, I think you'll find quite a number of people who have been growing uneasy about Angus. Quite a few people have been wondering if he isn't past it. Cracks notes. Unreliable. I'm not the only one to suffer.'

'You just name them!' Angus snarled furiously. 'You just tell me who says so, and I'll spread them all round the car park, after I've spread your lip all round your face.'

'Yes, well, that would appeal to you as the solution, wouldn't it?' Ivor drawled. 'But I'm afraid there are some things that can't be remedied as easily as a pub brawl.'

'You're being deliberately provocative,' Annie said, trying to keep herself between Angus and his tormentors. 'If you've any serious complaints to make, you should bring them up before the Board. And if you haven't, you should keep your mouth shut, and save your wind for blowing your horn.'

'It's easy to see where your loyalties lie,' Ivor said to her, his eyes narrowing, 'and it isn't with the orchestra. I suppose you'd stick up for any cur dog that came sniffing round you –'

He said no more than that, because Angus's fist with all his thirteen stone behind it lashed out like a mule's hind foot and silenced him. Some musician's instinct made Angus hit him in the stomach rather than the face. Ivor sat down abruptly with an *oof*! and clutched his diaphragm, speechless, while Angus stood over him, suddenly calm.

'And now you've gone too far, laddie, too far altogether. When ye've yer breath back, ye can apologise to the lady, and then ye can get out. Unless ye want me tae use yer bawdie as a bolster?'

'All right, all right, what's going on here?' came the rich, confident tones of Doris Walker, arriving on the scene with a nose for a scandal. 'Who's hitting who? Ivor, what've you been saying now? I've warned you to stop stirring it. And you, Angus, you ought to be ashamed of yourself, hitting a kid like him. You ought to know he can't help himself.'

'He insulted Annie,' Angus said, looking, unaccountably, as though he *were* ashamed of himself.

'Well, that's very naughty of him, but I dare say Annie can take care of herself, can't you, love? Up you get, Ivor, you're not dead yet. Why don't you two go out and get some fresh air in your lungs. A nice healthy walk might put you in a healthier frame of mind.' This last was to Glyn and Ivor, Glyn having helped Ivor to his feet.

More people were arriving on the scene now, and it was threatening to turn into a farce.

'I'm afraid there'll be no healthy walks for anyone this morning, bar the big brass – there's an extra rehearsal,' Annie said, and explained the situation. 'I'd better get on with telling the others, before they start going out.' And to crown the moment, the waiter arrived exactly then with Annie's forgotten breakfast. She felt her lips twitching with suppressed laughter, and catching Angus's eye just then, it all burst out. Doris continued to look grave.

'You've bitten off more than you can chew, if you think you can take Jekyll and Hyde on,' she said, meaning Glyn and Ivor, who had left the room. 'There'll be trouble from that quarter, you mark my words.'

But Annie was too busy bolting her food down to take much heed. 'A good breakfast spoiled,' she muttered as she dashed off to start phoning the musicians' rooms. By the time Ted appeared, washed, shaved, freshly dressed, hungry, and looking forward to a day out somewhere with his new love, the excitement was all over, and Annie was already on her way to the town hall.


Most of the orchestra dashed off after the Sunday concert in order to spend the night at home, rather than travel up very early the next day, there being a session in the afternoon at which all of them would be wanted. One of those who did not rush off was Gordon Wilson, a fiddler, who was celebrating his engagement to an American heiress, and was throwing a party after the concert to which Ted, among others, was invited, along with his second trumpet, Andy Wayne. It was only in the interval of the concert that Gordon got round to asking Annie, and she was not prepared for it.

'Thanks all the same, but I think I'd sooner get back to town. I've got heaps of washing to do, and if I don't do it tomorrow morning, God knows when I'll have time.'

'A poor excuse, Holst,' Gordon said – he had the ex-public-schoolboy's trick of using surnames. 'Old Willment will be disappointed.'

Oh God, Annie thought, is it spreading already? 'Why?' she asked sharply. Gordon didn't seem to notice her acerbity.

'He was the one who thought of asking you. Distinct lack of females in this part of the world. I think the Swanseaites must have locked up their daughters when they heard the orchestra was in town. Can't imagine why.'

Annie grinned. 'Nor can I! Thanks anyway, Gordie. Have you thought of asking the other girls?'

'Already have,' he said. 'All coming except Walker – she's got to get back to hubby. Oh well, if you won't, you won't. Have fun with the suds.'

Annie had come down by train, not caring much for long drives, but she was destined to go back in better style, for shortly after Gordon had wandered away, Angus came up with the air of one who has been searching.

'Ah, there you are. Listen, are you going to Gordon Wilson's bunfight?'

'No, I want to get back home. I've a ton of washing to do.'

'Will you do me a favour, then?' She nodded. 'Will you come back with me in the car. I hate driving alone, especially at night. It won't take much longer than the train, and I'll take you right to your door.'

'Okay, Angus, thanks. That'll suit me fine,' she said, though privately she wondered if driving was quite safe with Angus. Even now he had a double Scotch in one hand and a glass of beer in the other. Still, he managed to play all right. After the nasty insinuations that had been thrown about at breakfast, Annie took the trouble to listen carefully during

53

the concert, concentrating on Angus, and she could not detect anything that might indicate he was playing less well than usual. She concluded that Ivor and Glyn were merely being bitchy, and wondered why it was they had picked on Angus. Was it because he had been sitting with her? Ivor certainly had it in for her. It made life very awkward. The OA was supposed to get on with everyone, and if it hadn't been for Doris Walker that morning, what more might have been said?

Angus drove a very distinctive Triumph Stag, and he drove it very fast. After a nervous first fifteen minutes, Annabel saw that he drove very well, none the less for driving fast, and settled down to enjoy it. The roads were clear, growing more empty as the night extended, and Angus chatted to her pleasantly about nothing in particular, obviously being one of those drivers who can't bear to drive in silence.

At around midnight he pulled off the motorway and drove along the old road for a time until he came to an all-night café, where he stopped.

'I don't know about you, but I'm starving,' he said. 'Let's get a cup of coffee and something to eat. I know this place – always stop here when I'm going to or from Wales. See the lorries? That's always a good sign. Not if they're foreign lorries, though – that might mean it's only their first trip.'

Inside the café the yellow light was welcoming, and the air was warm and steamy and redolent of chips. The blackness seemed to press up against the windows, impatient to encroach. Half a dozen lorry drivers were sitting at the tables over great mugs of tea, and two of them were playing dominoes, while their dog, a black and white collie, dozed with its head on the feet of one and its tail on the feet of the other.

'Hello, Angus, you back again? Hello, dear,' the woman behind the counter greeted them as they went in. The heads all went up, Annie and Angus were scrutinised, and the heads went down again. 'What's it to be, then?'

'Hello, Mary, how's tricks? What would you like, Annie?'

'I'm not actually hungry,' Annie said. 'Can I just have tea?'

'Of course. Two teas, please, Mary, and I'll have – let's see – sausage, egg and chips.'

'Right you are, dear. Any bread with it?'

'Yes, please.'

'Just going, or just coming back?' Mary asked as she poured the tea and plonked the bread and butter on a plate.

'Just coming back. Giving a lift to this young lady – new recruit.'

'Nice to meet you, dear,' the woman flashed a smile at Annie. 'You take care of this bloke, now, he's a real gent. You'll be all right with him. That's what I tell all the hitchhikers. I wouldn't like to see a daughter of mine hitching, but I always say to any that come in – you'll be all right with him.'

At their table, Annie said, 'She seems to have a high opinion of you.'

'Oh, I did her a good turn once.' He wouldn't have said any more, but Annie pressed him, and he admitted, reluctantly, 'I took care of a bloke that was giving her a hard time in here one night.'

'Goodness, rescuing ladies seems to be your forte,' Annie said. 'I must say, though, I think you're very brave. I'm terrified of physical violence.'

'It's not brave really. It's what you're used to. Where I come from, it's like second nature to go in with your fists flying. I remember my Dad saying to me, there should never be more than one punch thrown in a fight, and that had better be yours.'

'I still think it's brave. Angus, why do you drink so much?'

He looked at her in surprise that she should ask so blunt a question, but seeing no malice in her face he said, 'The usual reason. To drown my sorrows.'

'What sorrows? Why are you unhappy?'

There was a silence as Mary brought his meal over, but once she had left them alone again, his confidence seemed to return, and bit by bit, as he ate, he told Annie his story.

55

He had married very young, to a girl from his own street.

'We were all Catholics, you see, and everything was kept very tight and insular. You were expected to marry young, and you always married someone your family knew, someone from the same small area. And you settled down and lived a few streets away, and in time your kids would marry the kids of someone you knew – and so it went on. Kathy was a good sort of girl, but we weren't alike.'

Their interests at seventeen had seemed similar but they gradually grew apart.

'I developed and she didn't – she stayed the same, mentally, as she had been when I first met her. Then there were other pressures. I didn't want to be laden down with kids. And music didn't pay well in those days. She and her folks were always at me to get a "proper job" so that I could buy her the clothes and the three-piece suites she wanted.'

After their second child they had moved to London, and things had seemed better for a while. Away from the influence of her family and the area she was born in, she was more easy to persuade by Angus. But she got lonely and bored away from her own people, and nagged and complained incessantly. 'So I started to go to pubs instead of going home. And that's where it started. And then the inevitable happened, I suppose – I fell in love with a girl.'

He had been giving lessons to augment his income, and he fell in love with one of his young students. He wanted to do everything properly, but when it came to it, his wife wouldn't give him a divorce.

'I would have treated her well, but Kathy was a Catholic, and that was that. And my girl was a very good girl, and she didn't just want to have an affair. Not that I would have wanted that for her either. I wanted the best for her. In the end, it was no good, and we parted.'

'What happened to her?'

Angus looked at her with agonised eyes. 'She fell foul of another bloke, less scrupulous than me. Or more attractive. I don't know. She had a baby, anyway, and the bloke couldn't marry her and wouldn't help her. She gave the baby away, and went abroad. Last I heard she was teaching in Hong Kong. That was years ago, though. All I could think was, if she'd given in to me, or if I'd been harder on her, at least that wouldn't have happened. I'd have stayed with her for ever. She wouldn't have had to give the kid away.'

There was a silence, and then he looked up and, seeing the tears in Annie's eyes, said, 'I shouldn't upset you. I'm a selfish bastard.'

'I asked,' Annie said. 'I'm so sorry.'

'Yes, I think you are,' he said quietly, as if surprised. 'Well, you're a nice girl. Now you know why I drink so much. I dare say it will kill me in the end, and no one'll be much sorry. Even my kids don't like me – their mother makes sure of that. Anyway, let's forget about it. Have some more tea? No? Then shall we get going? And don't ask me questions like that again – once I start I don't know where to stop.'

They stood up, and Annie slipped her arm through his and squeezed it affectionately. 'You're a nice man. I like you. Don't apologise for anything.'

He smiled back at her, and then, as if on an uncontrollable whim, he leaned forward and kissed her on her forehead. Companionably, they hit the road again.

By the time they got to Annie's flat, it was very late – or early, depending which way you looked at it – and they were very tired. Angus's place was on the other side of London still, and there seemed no point in sending him away at that time, so Annie put him up on the sofa in her sitting-room. She was just dozing off into a tumbled and confused sleep, when Angus came padding in, fumbling over the bed in the dark for her hand. His was icy cold, and he was shaking.

'Annie,' he whispered hesitantly, 'can I come in with you? Not to do anything, but just for the company?' She didn't immediately answer, and he was withdrawing his hand with a sigh that sounded half sick, and she was ashamed of her own hard-heartedness. She caught his hand back and lifted the covers, and with a little sound of relief he slipped in beside her and snuggled his cold body up against her.

She put an arm over him, and stroked his head tentatively,

57

not knowing quite what he meant to do, but he seemed really only to want company, and, still holding her hand, he fell asleep. A little while later he had a nightmare and woke her shouting and struggling. She sat up and put the light on, and he came to wakefulness, shocked and wide-eyed.

'It's all right,' she said, 'it was only a dream. I'm here.' He stared at her uncomprehendingly, but bit by bit he calmed down, and she put the light out again and lay down, and when she took him back into her arms, he broke at last, and put his head on her shoulder, and cried.

In the morning when she woke, he had gone, but there was a note, scribbled on the back of an envelope, lying on the pillow beside her head.

'Thanks, Pal,' it said. 'You're a woman seldom found.'

# FIVE

The next few weeks were very pleasant for Annie, for she had found a niche for herself at last. Everyone in the orchestra, with the exception of Ivor Hotchkiss, got on well with her, and she had two firm friends in Ted and Angus. Nothing was said by either of them about what had passed between them, and she was glad of it, for at the moment she had no wish to commit herself more firmly to anyone or anything; but during coffee-breaks and after sessions it was with them she spent her spare time. After concerts when the players scattered to their homes or to pubs, Annie would generally find herself invited in a most casual, friendly way, to join up with them, in a group that included Andy Wayne and David Bastowe and one or two other people of like mind.

The evening would then be lively, with plenty of talk, gossip, jokes and drinks, and at the end of it sometimes Ted would come with her, and sometimes she would go home alone; sometimes she would ask him in, and they would make love, and it was as terrific as it had been the first time. But always afterwards he would go home to sleep – it seemed that to have stayed the night would have suggested some kind of commitment, and in all courtesy he would not ask for that commitment until she offered it of her own free will. Annie understood the scrupulousness of that courtesy, and was grateful for it.

One day during the coffee-break at a rehearsal Annie came into the bar and looked round for her usual companions, and saw them sitting together in a corner with their heads together. She smiled to herself as she went over to join them. Put a lot of men together, and what you got was a schoolboy atmosphere of pranks and practical jokes, she thought – and never let anyone say that women were gossips! Men were a hundred times as bad.

'I've got a bit of news for you,' she said as she reached the group. The heads came up, and room was automatically made for her, Andy Wayne getting up to give her his seat while he foraged for another for himself. Annie smiled her thanks, and said, 'It's about the concert in Leicester – they want "The Rite of Spring", no less, and damn the expense.'

'Well that'll put a few smiles on a few faces,' said Ken Clarke, a fiddler from Birmingham who was one of their clique. 'Everybody likes the "Rite" – good parts for everyone.'

'Not to say all the extra musicians,' Annie said. 'And it'll mean two extra rehearsals, my children, which is all money.'

'I'd sooner have the time off than the money,' David Bastowe complained. 'I still haven't finished decorating the lounge.'

'And you never will, my child,' Ted said solemnly. 'To my certain knowledge you've been meaning to re-paper that room for the last four years.'

'Well, when do I ever get the time?' David said. 'I made sure I was getting a day and a half off next week. Why on earth do they want to do the "Rite?"'

'Job creation scheme,' suggested Andy Wayne, coming back with his chair. 'Part of the government's drive to bring down unemployment in the Midlands.' Everyone laughed at that – 'The Rite of Spring' was notorious for needing a full orchestra plus a large number of extra players as well.

'Delusions of grandeur, I think,' Annie replied. 'They're under the impression that it will show them up for daring, *avant-garde* trend-setters. But what was it you were all so busy talking about when I came in? You looked as if you were plotting something.'

'Our downfall,' someone muttered. She looked from one face to another and saw that it wasn't good news.

'What's happened?' she asked.

'Ivor Bloody Hotchkiss has happened,' Ted said at last. 'He's been elected to the Board, and that's what I call Bad News.'

'Elected to the Board?' Annie was puzzled. 'But how? Who would vote for him?'

'Lots of people,' Angus said, staring gloomily into his

mid-morning whisky. 'He's a bright young go-ahead junior executive – lots of people love the type.'

'Well, why didn't you all vote against him? Surely there must be more of you than of them.'

'Look, pussy-cat,' Angus began, and Ted interrupted with, 'There are basically two types of players – the political and the non-political.'

'We'll call them Exhibit A and Exhibit B,' someone mocked his style of rhetoric, but he ignored them.

'The non-political just want to play, and all they care about is the end result of the music. The political like to get involved with internal politics, the administrative side of our lives. And when it comes to an election, the political mob vote for one of their own kind, and the non-political crowd don't bother to vote at all, because they aren't interested in that kind of thing. And if they did vote, they'd have to vote for someone political because someone non-political wouldn't want to stand for election anyway.'

'Thank you, Professor,' David Bastowe said. 'And next week, in our series of Talks by the Experts –'

'Yes, all right, I get the picture,' Annie said. 'It's the same kind of thing in universities, with the students' union. Well, there doesn't seem to be much anyone can do about it, does there?'

'It won't necessarily be a bad thing anyway,' Ken Clarke said. 'He's got lots of useful contacts. If the Board makes him chairman, I dare say he might do a lot of good for the orchestra.'

'Starting, we hope, with providing a few extra women around here,' said David. 'The two vacancies we still have could easily be filled by women –'

'You bored with the ones we have?' Ken Clarke asked.

'Old Ivor isn't that liberal,' Andy Wayne put in. 'Your young executive types never are.'

And Angus and Ted exchanged a glance, which Annie intercepted, and she understood. With the power he had told them would one day be his, what would Ivor Hotchkiss do to Angus?

Ivor celebrated his rise to power by spraining a finger on the eve of the Leicester concert, leaving Annie with an almost impossible task.

'How the hell can I replace him?' she raved to Angus and Ted as she paused to drink a cup of coffee standing up.

'Do sit down and drink that, you'll give yourself indigestion,' Ted said. 'Anyway, all your rushing around makes me tired.'

'I have to rush around,' she said, 'there's a panic on.' But she sat down all the same, compromising by sitting on the very edge of her chair to be able to rise the more quickly when she had finished.

'What's the panic?' Angus asked, tipping the last drops of his whisky into his black coffee in his thrifty Scottish way. 'Don't say Tony's little black book has let you down?'

This was the address book with the names of all the players who could be contacted when extras were needed which each OA kept and added to and passed on with the job.

'Not exactly let me down,' Annie said, 'but I'd used up all the names for extras anyway. Why did they have to choose the bloody old "Rite?" And all the other orchestras seem to be doing Bruckner and Shostakovitch and people like that who all need extra horns too.'

'Let me look, something might strike me,' Angus said, holding out his hand, and reluctantly Annie passed the book across.

'It won't do any good, I've rung everybody I can think of,' she sighed. Angus flicked through.

'Did you try Trevor Wells?'

'Yes. He's busy.'

'Hm. Hm. Hm.' Ted caught her eye and grinned as Angus turned pages with a frown of concentration. Annie shrugged and smiled back reluctantly.

'Delia Gooden? Laurence James?'

'I've got them already.'

'What about Geoffrey Hamilton?' He looked up quickly as he said the name, in time to see her jerk of surprise, in time to see her face blanch. She got hold of herself quickly.

'He's a principal, Angus, he'll hardly be free.'

'Did you try?' Angus insisted. 'Because I happen to know that he always takes his holidays at this time, and he might be quite glad of an extra session. And it is a first you want.'

'Not necessarily,' she said. 'Barry can take the first's part, so a third would do.'

'I can see it's no good arguing with you,' Angus said, standing up, 'so I'll go and ring him myself.'

'No, don't –' Annie began, but Angus got up remarkably nimbly for him and was off to the telephone before she could say anything else.

'Never mind old Angus,' Ted said gently, 'he needs something to keep him occupied. He's been thinking too much these past few days.'

Annie nodded, but was unable to think of anything to say. Angus was soon back, looking pleased with himself.

'All fixed up,' he announced. 'You see, I've saved your reputation, and I've also saved poor Barry from having to play first, which I know he hates. But I don't expect any thanks. Virtue hath its own reward. True charity is anonymous.'

'Thanks, Angus,' she said, and if he noticed she didn't sound very grateful, he didn't say so.

The afternoon session finished early to help those who wanted to travel up to Leicester that night. Ted sought Annie out at the end of the session and offered to drive her home.

'I'm not going up until tomorrow morning, so if you were thinking of travelling tomorrow as well, we could go up together and save petrol,' he said.

'Okay, thanks,' she said. 'Shall we have dinner tonight? Or are you busy.'

'If I were, I'd cancel it,' he said, taking her hand and pressing it. 'But I hoped you might feel like going out somewhere. I think we both need a bit of a break.'

'You don't know how true that is,' she said.

'Perhaps I do,' he replied. 'Shall I choose? Shall we eat fairly early, so we can get an early night? How about seven o'clock?'

'That will suit me,' she said. 'Where?'

'I know a really marvellous little place in the Fulham Road, called Provans. Have you ever been there? It's only about ten minutes from your flat.' Annie lived in Chelsea. 'I'll pick you up at a quarter to, all right?'

Annie had never been to Provans, and when she got there she was not surprised she didn't know it, because it was almost invisible from the road. The restaurant was upstairs in a long, narrow building set end-on to the street. It was a small room, and there were lots of tables in it, but once they were seated it was surprising how private one felt; and the lighting and decor were pleasant and unremarkable so that nothing distracted one from a cosy tête-à-tête.

'You look very beautiful tonight,' Ted said, taking her hand across the table. Annie looked into his dark eyes and felt herself relaxing, the tensions of the past few days melting away. 'Is that a new dress? I haven't seen it before.'

'Not new,' she said. 'I've had it for some time, but I always think of it as my best dress, so I don't wear it much.'

'So I merit your best dress? I'm flattered,' he said. It was a rose-pink crêpe de Chine dress, with wide, loose sleeves reaching to the elbow, and a lot of ribbons and lace on the bodice. 'You should wear pink more often, it suits you. You look like the princess in fairy tales – they always had golden hair and wore pink silk dresses on their birthday. And rosebuds in their hair. And that was the day they met the prince who was to change their lives, of course.'

'I haven't any rosebuds,' Annie smiled. 'And I'm afraid I met the prince years ago, and he *did* change my life. I don't think I'd want to go through that again.'

He looked suddenly serious. 'I know about Geoffrey Hamilton,' he said. She stared and tried to withdraw her hand, but he held on to it. 'Don't be angry. I don't want to pry. I just wanted you to know I know.'

'How?' she asked at last. He shrugged.

'It wasn't entirely a secret, you know,' he said. 'Quite a lot of people knew. Amongst them, of course, Bob Akroyd.'

'Who else knows?' she asked.

64

'Among our lot? I don't know. No one I should think. It isn't a thing one discusses, you know. But I knew Bob very well, and of course –'

'Of course,' she said harshly. She looked up and met his eye defiantly. 'Well?'

'Well,' he said. 'Do you want to talk about it?'

'I thought you knew everything,' she said, trying to hurt.

'Not your story,' he said gently. His eyes were the darkest, kindest, deepest pools she had ever longed to drown herself in.

'Not now,' she said, almost pleadingly. 'Later. Tonight.' He nodded.

'All right. We'll enjoy our meal, talk nonsense. Don't tell me anything you don't want to.'

'I won't,' she said. 'I can't think of anything I wouldn't want to tell you. You are a very remarkable man, you know. One feels instinctively one can trust you.'

'Does one?' he laughed.

'*I* do,' she said firmly. 'Let's have a lot of wine and a lot of food, a real Roman orgy.'

They had a wonderful meal and then, slightly, pleasantly tipsy, went back to Annie's flat. She opened the door and Ted followed her in, reaching for the light switch, but she caught his hand before it made contact and drew him to her.

'No,' she said, 'We don't need the light. I can find my way in the dark.'

'Find your way where?' he asked teasingly, responding to her automatically – it was not a thing over which he had any control.

'All over you,' she said. She kissed him lightly on the lips. 'Come on,' she said, pulling him by the hand towards the bedroom. 'Sex first, talk afterwards. Come and make love to me. You can't imagine how I want you.'

'Can't I?' he said. In the bedroom, lit dimly by the street lights outside, they undressed each other carefully, never moving more than an inch apart, their breathing becoming more laboured as if this pleasant task were hard work. Then, moving in harmony like ballroom dancers, they lay down upon the bed and wrapped their arms around each other.

'I see what you mean,' she said. 'Or rather, I feel what you mean. Ted?'

'Mm? I thought you said talking was for afterwards.'

His mouth was against hers. 'I'm not really talking,' she murmured into it.

Their mood was languorous, almost melancholy. They made long, slow love, and in spite of their great desire for each other, they made it last a long time. Ted was even rather surprised at his own control. They caressed each other almost into a stupor; but nothing lasts for ever. The long, slow climb brought them at last to the top of the hill, and they were racing together down the short, sharp, exhilarating slope on the other side. Ted heard himself cry out softly, almost in disappointment – it *ought* to be possible to go on for ever. Annie made little soft whimpering noises; and then it was all over, and they were clapsed together; sweaty, limp, exhausted, but with a sense of having achieved something together. Annie felt a rush of affection for her friend, and she hugged him hard in the darkness. Ted felt more than that, but he knew it was not the time to say it. He returned her hug with a kiss, turned on the bedside lamp, and lay down again, drawing her onto his shoulder and folding his arms round her, and they lay like that for a long time, contented with each other, smiling.

They must have fallen asleep for a time, for Ted woke abruptly and saw that it was nearly half-past ten. He tried to ease himself out from under her, and she woke too.

'What is it?' she said, struggling up onto her elbows.

'It's all right. I was just thinking I'd better be going. It's getting late.'

Annie smiled at him, glancing at the clock. 'So scrupulous, my dear friend,' she said. 'One would imagine you had never even thought of staying the night.'

He looked grave. 'Until you invited me –'

'I know. Really, I do appreciate it. But Highgate is an awful long way. I would be glad of the company, if you would stay the night. Then we could make an early start tomorrow. Please, sleep with me?'

He smiled, transforming his face. She thought with a pang that when he smiled like that he was really beautiful. 'I'd like nothing better,' he said. 'But what about a cup of tea now? Making love makes me thirsty.'

'Not to speak of all that wine. Yes, let's have a cup of tea – you put the kettle on while I wash. We'll have it in the kitchen.'

And so it was in the kitchen, sitting on the high stools at the breakfast bar and drinking fragrant cups of Earl Grey, that The Talk finally occurred – that Annie finally told him the story of Geoffrey Hamilton.

Annie had fallen in love with Geoffrey Hamilton the first time she had seen him, when she was only eighteen. He was tall, dark, elegant and handsome – anyone would have fallen for him. Annie was petite, honey-fair, with an English rose complexion and fine grey eyes, and together they made what nannies call a 'lovely couple'. Annie was not thinking of making any kind of couple with him at that time – she was in love with him as one is in love with a film star – he was her pin-up. She never expected to get any nearer to him than that, and probably, deep in her heart, she didn't want to. For her at the time music was all.

Nothing happened for a couple of years. They met from time to time on the music circuit, and were acquainted, that was all. Then came the summer of her great triumph, when she did a series of concerts with Geoffrey's orchestra. The English Sinfonietta had always had a reputation for helping young talented people in their careers, but even so Annie was so thrilled she could hardly take it in. It was such a huge step from the Wigmore Hall to the Festival Hall, and playing with a full orchestra felt to her rather like driving a huge truck – so much power, and not at all under her control.

The concerts were a success. Annie was launched on what promised to be a great career as a violinist. Julie, then just

67

married to Pat, was predicting all manner of likely and unlikely things. And Annie was radiant with success and love, for she had re-met, and got to know, Geoffrey Hamilton, and all through that wonderful summer she was his mistress.

She had never had a lover before, so to all the other experiences were added the feelings of a passionate young girl towards the man who first makes love to her. Geoffrey Hamilton was a skilled lover. Annie was very deeply in love, not doubting that it would last for ever, assuming that in the fullness of time they would marry, but never speaking of it, taking her lover's lead. She never wondered if Geoffrey felt the same way about her – she just assumed that he did, and it seemed so much beyond question that they should eventually marry that it never occurred to her to wonder why he didn't speak of it – she assumed he took it for granted as much as she did.

In the autumn came her tour of Israel and the Near East. She had a wonderful time, and returned flushed with triumph and longing to see Geoffrey again. She telephoned him on her very first evening back in London.

'Darling, there are so many things I have to tell you,' she bubbled over the phone.

'I have something to tell you, too,' he said. 'I'm married.'

'I can't describe to you how shocked I felt,' she told Ted. 'It seemed to me so horrible – the idea of him marrying someone else was almost obscene.'

The lady in question was even younger than Annie herself – the daughter of some friends of his parents. It was almost an arranged marriage, except that Annie very soon realised Geoffrey himself wanted it quite as much as any of the four parents could. It had all been decided quite a while ago. All though the summer while he had been making love to Annie, his future wife had been in a finishing school in Paris, only waiting for the term to end to come home and marry Geoffrey. He had known all the time.

Annie's pride sustained her, and prevented her from revealing to Geoffrey what her own expectations had been.

To salve her pride she had to pretend she had only been amusing herself with him, just as he had with her; and to keep up the fiction, she had resumed her position as his mistress almost as soon as he returned from his honeymoon.

'That wasn't the only reason, of course,' she admitted to Ted. 'I loved him so much it wasn't hard to persuade myself to it, though I must admit I did feel horribly guilty from time to time. And things went on like that for several months – until I got pregnant. That put the cat among the pigeons.'

Geoffrey had wanted her to have an abortion, and had offered to pay for it, but she would not hear of it.

'To tell you the truth, I was terrified. Quite apart from the thought that I couldn't possibly kill Geoffrey's child, I thought it would be far worse to go through an abortion than through childbirth. I just didn't have the guts. So then Geoffrey said he would get divorced and marry me, for the child's sake. I don't know if he really would have, or if he was just stalling. I never found out, you see, because there was a car accident. At a crossroads. A car drove straight into the side of Geoffrey's at high speed. Geoffrey was all right, but his wife was horribly injured. The car hit the passenger side, you see.'

There was no more talk of Annie's problem after that, and she could only wait in mute sympathy until the shock had died down. Shona, Geoffrey's wife, was in hospital for two months, and when she came out it was plain that there could be no more talk of divorce.

'She was paralysed from the waist down,' Annie said. 'It was terrible – she was so young, younger than me, and they'd hardly been married six months. Of course he had to stay with her then. He couldn't possibly have deserted her, even if he wanted to – and I don't think he did. So my problem became very much a second feature. I had to work it out for myself.'

Annie found herself trembling at that point in her narrative, and Ted was discreet enough to attribute it to cold. 'Come on, let's get into bed. You can finish the story there – or leave it till another time, as you please.'

69

'I'll finish it,' she said. 'There isn't much more to tell.' They switched off the lights and got into bed, and Ted put his arms round her, and in the comforting, all-concealing darkness, she told him the last bit of the sad story.

She had decided long ago to have the baby, but she didn't know of any way she could keep it. She had no money and no home – she lived in a bedsit at the time. Her only relative was Julie, and Julie and Pat were then struggling for every penny, they certainly couldn't come to her aid.

'Not only that,' she said, 'but I thought of my career. It sounds selfish, I know, but somehow you can't think much about a baby until it comes – it doesn't seem much like a person when you haven't had one before. I thought if I kept the baby, I'd have to give up my career – and I didn't want to do that. So I told Geoffrey that I'd give the baby away, have it adopted.'

Geoffrey had thoroughly approved – it seemed the best idea all round. They had not seen much of each other during the last months of her pregnancy, for he had been too occupied with caring for his crippled wife and reorganising his life around her needs, trying to square them with the time-consuming nature of his profession. Annie had gone into a mother-and-baby home for the last few weeks, and had her baby there, and they said that they would arrange for the adoption as well, if she still wanted it when the baby was born.

The baby was born – a boy. She called him Sacha. 'It was a very popular name then,' she said apologetically. Ted squeezed her in acknowledgment. 'Geoffrey came and visited me there when the baby was a fortnight old, and asked me if I still wanted to give the child up. I was hesitant, because they get you, once they've arrived, they're so helpless it seems somehow callous to pass them around like brown-paper parcels. But I still wanted to follow my career, so I said yes, I did. And he said then, would I give the baby to him and Shona.'

It had been Shona's idea. She had found out about Annie and her condition a few days before the baby was born, and

70

Geoffrey had told her the whole story, or at least a version of it he thought suitable. And then she had said, why didn't they adopt the baby? She herself could never have children, and Geoffrey would be sure to want them some day, and this way at least the child would have one real parent. Also, it would be hard for a crippled woman to adopt through the normal channels, if not impossible, so it seemed like a good answer to everyone's problems.

'It seemed logical – so logical, one could hardly fight against it,' Annie said soberly into the darkness. 'To cut a long story short, we talked about it, and in the end I agreed. Geoffrey did all the legal bits, all I had to do was sign the paper and hand the baby over. It was decided that Shona and I should never meet. I don't think she even knew my name. He took the baby, and I went back to my career. It didn't last long. Six months later I had a nervous breakdown, and after that, I just couldn't play any more. I tried and tried, but whatever it was I'd had, it had gone. I've never played a note since. So now you know all.'

She stopped talking, and in the darkness waited for Ted's reaction. He said nothing for a long time, and she wondered if he had gone to sleep during her long boring narrative. But at last he gave a long sigh, and kissed her forehead, and said, 'I knew some of it. Not the details. Of course, he never said anything – it was only what was picked up and passed on by various people. You've never seen the child since?'

She shook her head.

'Very wise,' he said. 'It would hardly have been fair.'

She didn't ask to whom. She was glad he didn't offer her sympathy. While telling the story, she had thought she wanted sympathy, but she realised now she did not. It all seemed so remote now, as if telling it had removed its power to hurt.

'I've never told anyone before,' she said. 'You're the first.'

'I'm glad,' he said. 'I'd like to be the first for everything. Let's sleep now. We'll talk some more tomorrow. Sleep, my darling.' He kissed her and rolled her over on her side, settling against her back spoon-wise, and folding a protective arm across her. She kissed his hand and smiled comfortably.

'Goodnight,' she murmured.

'Goodnight, Annie. I love you very much.'

# SIX

Annie was standing backstage with her head bent over one of her lists, checking off names, when a voice said behind her, 'Miss Holst, I believe? No relation to Gustav?'

A voice so familiar it was like a physical touch, and the words he had always used, a private joke between them. She turned so abruptly she almost banged her nose on him.

'Hello,' he said. He looked just the same, except that there was more grey in his hair. Feeling her jaw sagging inelegantly, she searched her mind for a riposte.

'Hello,' she said. She had always been famous for her repartee.

'Here you are, then,' he said at length.

'Yes,' she said. How long could they keep this up? 'How are you?'

'Oh, just the same. You know me. Never a day's illness in my life.'

'You look well.'

'So do you. This job must be suiting you.'

'It was. I mean, it is. And I must get on with it, if you'll excuse me.' Determinedly, she dragged herself away. Her bones were beginning to turn to water, and she did not want to remain in his presence for too long. Like Superman in the presence of green kryptonite. He radiated all sorts of things that were bad for her. She made her escape, and, typically of him, he called her to a halt as she was about to disappear.

'How about tasting the delights of Leicester with me at lunch-time?'

She turned and looked at him, managing to hold herself together for long enough to say, 'I don't really think so, Geoffrey. Anyway, I'll be busy then.' He did not seem either surprised or put out by her refusal. He was smiling slightly in that way that made her think he had known what she was going to say before she said it. He had always done that to

73

her. As she scuttled to safety she found herself thinking that it had always infuriated her, which was simply not true. In the old days it used to impress and disarm her.

At lunch-time Angus hauled her off for a drink, and she allowed herself to be hauled.

'First meeting safely over, then,' he said as he put her drink in front of her. She stared at him in amazement.

'God, not another one! Is there anybody, tell me, who doesn't know about me and Geoffrey?'

'Well, I didn't know,' Angus admitted easily. 'I was just putting the odd two and two together. So there was something between you two?'

'"Something" just about describes it,' Annie said. Angus assumed an expression of deep gloom.

'Bloody horn-players. I don't know why you wanted to get mixed up with one. Like flies and critics, there's no excuse for 'em.'

'Oh, what has your particular fly been doing recently?'

'Nothing much. We circle each other stiff-legged, hackles raised and teeth bared. The trouble is, he knows I don't mean it and I know he does.'

'Maybe his power-complex will die once he gets used to being saviour of the world,' Annie said. 'Talking of saviours –' She caught sight of Ted looking round for them, and waved, and he came over.

'So here you are,' he said, pretending to be aggrieved. 'What are you doing?'

'Stealing your woman,' Angus said laconically. 'Wanna make somethin' of it?'

'She's yours for a double Scotch,' Ted said, sitting down. Angus got up and went to the bar, and Ted took the opportunity to take hold of Annie's hand under the table and squeeze it.

'All right?' he asked her. She smiled and nodded. 'No, really – he hasn't said anything to you? You aren't feeling too bad about it?'

'Nothing happened. I can withstand the blast for a short time without completely caving in, I think.'

74

'Good girl. Chin up. Throw out your chest – you won't need it. Take it like a man. Over the top, sergeant, I'm right behind you.'

'All right, all right, I get the general idea. But look, Ted –'

'What is it, darling one?'

'After the concert tonight, will you buttonhole me, stick close to me, and whisk me away as soon as possible. If I'm not taken care of, I'm afraid he'll ask me to go with him, and one brainless part of me is longing to ask him all sorts of questions.'

'Consider yourself buttonholed, stuck close to, and whisked, ' Ted said.

'Thanks.'

But what devil was it that prompted her to wear her Zandra Rhodes dress that night, softly crinkled black Indian cotton edged with cotton-lace, full skirted, low-cut, a mixture of the demure and wicked? Even Ted, who must be used to her looks by now, raised an eyebrow at her, and Ivor gave her a glare of pure homicide. Tell herself what she might, it must have been for Geoffrey's benefit she did it, because when he came up behind her, placed the breath of a kiss on the back of her neck, and said, with a luxurious sniff, 'Hmm, I see you still wear Balenciaga,' she wasn't at all surprised, only gratified and flattered. She turned to look at him, her heart hammering painfully.

'You approve?' she asked.

'You always had good taste, I'll say that for you,' he said. Their words were light, but their eyes devoured each other like starving people, and the looks they exchanged were full of the past and memories of an old love. Annie felt herself weakening, felt the beginnings of the crazy desire to throw herself into his arms and beg to be made love to; but she would not yet quite give in to the flood of memories that was pressing against the barrier she had put up in her mind. She dragged her gaze away from his familiar face, and made herself speak coolly.

'I must be about my work,' she said briskly. 'I'm glad

75

you're here on time – as I remember you always used to be last in the old days.'

'In the old days,' he reminded her with a faint smile, 'I was always with you, that's what made me late.'

She wouldn't remember, she *wouldn't* remember. She turned away abruptly and left him.

Her troubles were not over – Angus hadn't arrived. Discreetly she asked questions, trying to keep any breath of the worry from Ivor who, true to his paranoia, had come along to watch, and Glyn Paradine. She asked Ken Clarke, with whom he spent his time when he was not with Ted's group, but it seemed no one had seen him since she herself with Ted left him at the pub at lunch-time. They had gone off to get some food, but he had declined to join them. In desperation she slipped her coat on and dashed out to check that same pub – luckily it was only a hundred yards from the hall.

Her guess was right. She looked in all three bars, and was about to withdraw to rack her brains for another solution when he emerged from the gents' and sat down at the nearest table over a half-finished pint. She ran across to him.

'Angus, what are you doing here? Don't you realise what the time is?'

He looked up at here and smiled. Her heart sank. It was a dislocated sort of smile.

'Oh! Hello, Annie. How frightfully nice to see you, old boy. Sit down and have a drink with me. A little liquid sustenance to keep out the cold wind of disillusionment. A flagon of porter to—'

'Angus, shut up. Are you crazy? Why do you do these things? Look, there's just time to get back to the hall and changed. How drunk are you? Can you play?'

He drew himself up in injured dignity.

'Let me tell you that no one has ever seen me the worse for drink. Play? I could play spots off any man or woman in this pub. Clear a ring and I'll show you.'

'This is no time for a chorus from "The Day We Went to Rothesay",' Annie said, trying to keep the mood light. 'Do come one, old thing, we're waiting for you. No one's noticed yet – I just slipped out to look for you.'

'If no one's noticed, how can you say they're all waiting? That is a prevarication, a deviation from the normal veracity of your utterances –'

'Oh shut up, and come on,' she said abruptly, losing patience. She grabbed his arm and pulled, and almost to her surprise he got to his feet. He walked after her sulkily.

'I don't see why I should. I'm a marked man anyway. That Hotchprick is gunning for me – he'll see me damned, if it's the last thing he does. Ivor Hotprick. And Glyn Parazone – he's a sort of musical bleach, kills ninety-nine per cent of talent on contact – dead. Balls to 'em.'

'All right, if that's your mood, say balls to them,' Annie encouraged him. 'Why hand them success on a plate. They think they can get you – show them they're wrong.'

Angus patted her shoulders kindly. 'Good effort,' he said. 'I can see you've been reading the handbook – page four, how to humour drunks. But it's no good, ma wee pal, they're after me. They'll get me, you'll see. And when they do – no flowers, by request. You'll come to my funeral, won't you, pally? I can count on you?'

'You can count on me for friendship,' she said, trying to sound cheerful and brisk. 'The rest is nonsense, and you know it.'

He sighed but said no more. She managed to get him in unnoticed through the fire exit, and he slipped along to the dressing-room he used. Annie scuttled off and looked for Ted.

'Where've you been?' he asked. 'People have been looking all over for you.'

'Never mind, go and see to Angus, will you. He's in his dressing-room – make sure he gets changed and gets on stage.'

'Oh, God – drunk?'

'Fairly. I don't know what will come of this evening. Glyn's bound to notice.'

'Well, maybe he won't. Angus is marvellous, drunk or

77

sober. And he always smells of drink. Maybe Glyn won't think there's any difference.'

Ten minutes later Annie watched the conductor take the rostrum, and sighed a deep sigh of relief. All her ninety-five men and women were safely on the platform ready for the performance. The audience was filling the auditorium – the concert was sold out completely – and the conductor was lifting his baton to begin. She felt a bit like a coach who has just got her protégé to the starting-line and now can only hope for the best. The baton came down, and the first notes crashed out as if released by that movement. The ninety-five individuals with all their individual characteristics, their private lives known and unknown, their problems, peculiarities and proclivities, were welded by that movement into a single body without features. Annie might look anxiously towards Angus to see if there was any visible difference from his usual performance, might glance half unwillingly at Geoffrey to see how exactly the same as always he looked, damn him; but to the audience they were The Orchestra, a single entity, a music-making machine. With a last glance and a sigh, Annie went backstage to get herself some strong black coffee.

After the concert, Annie was talking to Warren Stacker and waiting for Ted to come and find her when they both pricked up their ears in anxiety at an outburst of angry voices coming from the region of the dressing-rooms.

'What the hell's that?' Warren asked. Annie listened for a second longer, and then ran.

'I don't know,' she flung over her shoulder, 'but it sounds like trouble.'

It was trouble. Forcing her way through the press of bodies who had gathered round either to help or to enjoy the spectacle she found Ivor, Glyn, Angus and Ted embroiled in a mill that would have been funny had it not been so serious. Angus was flailing about like a flounder on a jetty, trying, it seemed, to hit Ivor, who had blood on his face, apparently from a bleeding nose. Glyn was trying to hold Angus still, hanging on behind him like a child hanging on the back of a lorry, presumably so that Ivor could hit him in comfort, and Ted was torn between holding Ivor still and dragging Glyn off Angus.

Annie was thrust into this circle by the force of the bodies she had wormed through rather like a cork coming out of a bottle. She flung herself between Ivor and Angus and placed a hand on the chest of each and yelled at them to stop. The noise cut off abruptly, and the bodies squirmed against her hands for only an instant longer.

'What the hell are you playing at?' she demanded angrily. 'You're like a bunch of kids on a school outing. Don't you know the press is out there in the auditorium? What'll happen if they hear about this?'

There was silence as this was absorbed. She turned to Ivor, reached into his pocket for a handkerchief and put it to his nose. His hand came up and took it from her and he dabbed cautiously.

'What happened to you?' she asked him. He looked at the blood on his handkerchief as if he had never seen blood before.

'He hit me,' he said in a horrified squeak.

'On the nose? Let me see, give me the hanky – is your lip cut?' She wiped the blood away and examined his face while he kept pathetically still, rolling his eyes in horror. 'No, it's all right, it's only your nose. Tilt your head forward a little and just dab – don't rub it or wipe it or you'll keep it flowing. Just dab and it'll stop in a minute. It isn't broken.'

'No thanks to that drunken sot,' Glyn said, still holding Angus viciously tightly by the upper arms. Annie looked at Angus and saw the despair in his face. 'Let him go,' she said. 'He won't do anything now. What happened?'

'Angus hit him, that's what happened. He's drunk, came on stage filthy drunk, and afterwards attacked poor Ivor – what more do you want to know?'

'Angus?' Annie turned to him. He strugged. 'You must have had a reason.'

79

'Only the usual,' Angus said. 'That bastard has such a big mouth, I thought he might like a fat lip to go with it.'

Ted said, 'He was threatening Angus, and he lost his temper. Justifiable provocation, or whatever it's called.'

'I'll get you for it,' Ivor said sullenly through his handkerchief. He was glaring at Angus, and everything that had just been said and done might never have happened. It was as if they were alone together and the blow had just been struck. 'You're finished. I'll get you thrown out of this orchestra so fast your feet won't touch the ground. And don't think you'll get a job anywhere else, either. I've got influence. No one'll touch you with a barge-pole when I've made a few phone calls. I'll finish you this time, you Scotch bastard. You've had it.'

Angus made no reply. He did not even move. Annie looked at him, and saw in his face that he knew Ivor could do it. He looked like a man condemned to death.

'Oh shove it, Ivor,' Annie said briskly. 'Haven't you done enough for one night? I think you'd better get yourself off to the local hospital, let them have a look at you, just to be on the safe side. Do you want someone to go with you?' She jerked her head sharply at Ted, to tell him to get Angus off the scene, and bit by bit she dispersed the crowd, trying by talking normally to defuse the violent situation. Ted hustled Angus away, Ivor crept off with his face under his handkerchief, accompanied by Glyn, and the rest of them drifted away talking in low voices. Annie was left alone on the scene, until Andy Wayne came back and asked if she wanted a lift home – which was like his kind heart!

'No, thanks all the same, Andy – I think I'd better go along to the hospital and make sure Ivor's all right. We've got New York next week.'

'Okay, love,' he said, and turned to go, but looked back to say, 'Don't worry too much. You did your best. They make a lot of noise, but they don't often mean what they say.'

'Who don't?' Annie asked, smiling wryly. 'Those two, or musicians in general?'

'Men,' he said.

'Thanks,' she said. 'I'll try to remember that.'

The news was bad. Though Angus's punch hadn't split Ivor's lip, it had loosened three of his front teeth, and by the next day his mouth was as sore and swollen as his nose. He would certainly not be able to play soon enough to go to New York, and he was considering suing Angus for assault. He was certainly going to make him pay for the dental work he would have to have. Annie's sympathies were largely with Ivor on this occasion, for she knew the terror that haunted a wind-player when there was any threat to his mouth. Loss of teeth, even if they could be replaced with false ones, could mean a musician might never play again.

She had her own worries – since Ivor could not go to New York, she had to find another first horn. It seemed like the perversity of fate that Geoffrey should be available for that week. Annie struggled long and hard with her conscience. There was one other person she could have got, but he was not as good a player as Geoffrey, and in the end her conscience would not allow her to choose second best for the orchestra.

'Won't your little friends in the Sinfonietta miss you?' she asked Geoffrey tartly over the phone when she booked him. 'You seem to be absenting yourself a lot these days.'

'I'm bored with them,' Geoffrey said. 'I want a change. I want to move on now – I've been with them long enough, and they aren't playing as well as they used to.'

'Why not go solo?' she asked – it was what usually happened to good virtuoso orchestral musicians.

'This will sound like treason to you, but I think the horn is at its best in orchestral pieces. The solos are fun, but they aren't great music.'

'It does sound like treason,' Annie said, 'but I happen to agree with you. The only solo instrument I really like, apart from the violin, is the oboe.'

'Kid stuff,' he said scornfully. 'Stick to the violin.' She wondered afterwards how much he meant by that.

Ivor was not fit to play, but he was fit to attend a meeting of the Board. Ted rang her up with the news which he got on the hotline from Andy Wayne, who was also on the Board.

'They've sacked Angus,' he said angrily. 'The bastards. No one spoke up for Angus at all, except dear old Andy, and they shouted him down. Even Doris wouldn't put in a word for him. I'm afraid he went too far when he hit Ivor – they couldn't condone that.'

'I'm not surprised,' Annie said, 'but I'm very shocked. Do you think Ivor will do what he said – black Angus everywhere?'

'He's a bastard of the first water, I wouldn't be surprised,' Ted said. 'Poor old Angie – it's going to hit him terribly hard. I'd like to get my hands round Ivor's neck. He's a power-maniac – he's got a Hitler complex you could slice up and bottle. God knows what he's going to do next.'

Annie's usual visit to Julie and Pat did not go well either, because Julie kept saying, I told you so.

'I knew it would throw you in his path again,' she said. 'Now you're off to the States with him, and it will all start all over again.

'*Nothing* will start,' Annie said crossly. 'I wish you'd stop dramatising. He's one of ninety musicians and it's only for a short time. It's a temporary appointment.'

'He won't rest at that,' Julie said darkly. 'You mark my words, he's after you.'

'Oh don't be ridiculous,' Annie snapped. But even Pat told her to be careful.

'These holiday romances,' he said lightly, but she knew that he meant it.

'Nothing will happen,' she said again. 'Do stop worrying – I'm a big girl now.'

'That's what I'm worried about. It's time you got married – let some other man worry about you.'

'You don't mean to say *you* worry about me?'

'Incessantly,' Pat said, brushing up against her. 'You're on my mind all the time. I've had you on the tip of my tongue a hundred times –'

'Now don't start that double-entendre business,' she said, beginning, foolishly, to blush. 'Anyone would think –'

'Yes, anyone would. Stick to that nice trumpeter of yours,' Pat said, suddenly serious. 'From what you say he seems like a nice bloke.'

'But is that enough,' she asked. 'A nice bloke.'

'It's a hell of a good start,' Pat told her.


The day before they left for New York they had a final rehearsal in some rooms in Holborn that they used from time to time. Ted and Andy and David were sitting together drinking coffee ten minutes before the rehearsal was due to start, talking in low voices.

'That bastard's gone too far this time,' Ted was saying, talking as usual about Ivor Hotchkiss. 'He's started ringing round people telling them not to take on old Angus when he's done his notice. He just can't *do* that sort of thing.'

'Evidently he can,' Andy said. 'He's doing it.'

'I know – he seems to have the influence – but what I mean is, we can't *let* him. God, if it's going to start getting like that, we'd all better pack our instruments and go to the States. I mean, what kind of a life will it be if that sort of political influence can be used to ruin a good musician?'

'There have always been those sort of undercurrents,' Andy said, but David broke in, 'Yes, but they were very few, and they were only undercurrents. I know what Ted means. We ought to do something about Hotchkiss. He's getting too big for our boots.'

Just then Annie arrive.

'You're late,' Ted called to her. 'That isn't showing us a good example, is it?' Then he caught sight of her face, and half-rose from his seat. 'What's the matter? What's happened?'

Annie stopped by their table and looked at them wearily,

83

as if it was a great effort to concentrate or speak. She passed a hand across her face.

'The police phoned me this morning. That's why I'm late, I was talking to them. Angus killed himself last night. His landlady found him when she went up to clean his room.'

# SEVEN

New York. They were staying in a hotel on Fifty-ninth Street, not far from the Lincoln Center where they would be playing.

'I'm determined to see as much of the city as possible,' Annie said at breakfast. 'Who knows when I'll come here again?'

'You won't see much,' Ted said, drinking orange juice so iced it made your teeth ache. 'I was here once before and all I saw was the inside of a taxi.'

'You didn't try,' Annie accused him. 'Still, having been here before, you can at least tell me what to see.'

'I doubt it. Until yesterday I still thought the Empire State Building was the highest building in the world.'

'Oh. Isn't it?'

'Ignorant!' He batted her on the nose. 'No, apparently the World Trade Centre's higher – or rather, Cent*er*,' he corrected himself with a nod to her, 'and they have a restaurant up on the top floor that you have to be the Aga Khan or Jackie Kennedy to get a table in.'

'Don't tell me about the places I can't see, tell me about the places I can see.'

'For a start, the inside of the Philharmonic Hall, like the rest of us, kid. Have you finished your brekky? Because, though I hate to tell you, it's after nine.'

'Glory be, we'll be late!' Annie said, stuffing the last piece of Toasted English Muffin (which turned out to be like a kind of bap with currants in it, not in the least like a muffin) into her mouth and leaping up.

'That's what I've been trying to tell you,' Ted said calmly, following her at a more civilised speed.

Despite what Ted said, there was time in the afternoon, between the rehearsal and the concert, to sightsee and, despite his reluctance to put foot to pavement, Annie finally

85

persuaded him to accompany her. She wanted to keep busy and occupied so that she didn't think too much about Angus, who had been on her mind. Every time her brain relaxed for a moment, he would ambush her from the silence left by his lonely death. She was troubled, too, that she had promised him, even though it was in joke, to go to his funeral, and because she was here with the orchestra, she would have to break the promise. His wife had claimed the body, and would be doing the needful that week, while they were all away. It seemed a last twist of perversity in a fate that had hounded him all his poor life.

So they walked out on to Broadway, and strolled along it.

'Kindly stop singing, you're making a spectacle of me,' Ted said.

'I'm not singing,' Annie said.

'You're breathing and walking in time to it,' he said severely.

'All right, but I mean just think – here I am, walking along Broadway!'

'You've been abroad before,' he said. 'Why so excited?'

'Yes, of course I've been abroad before. But I haven't been to New York before. After all, it is the greatest city in the world – after London.'

Ted grinned and ruffled her hair. 'Don't let the natives hear you say that. We'd better get something to eat, anyway, before we do any serious gawping. What do you fancy?'

'Is there a delicatessen near by? Because I've always wanted to eat a hot pastrami on rye from a delicatessen.'

'You have the strangest ideas – why hot pastrami on rye?'

'I just like the sound of it. It *sounds* like New York to me. The way mutton pie and beans sound like Edinburgh.'

Ted laughed. 'You are lovely! All right, we'll get you a sandwich, and I'll even let you order it yourself. Actually, I think Zabars is somewhere up this way – we'll ask.'

'What's Zabars?' Annie asked.

'The most famous delicatessen in New York,' Ted said.

'How do you know? I thought you didn't know anything about here?'

'It's where Frank Sinatra has his sandwiches sent from when he's abroad,' Ted said. 'I read it somewhere. And what's good enough for Old Red Eyes is good enough for you. Excuse me –'

He stopped a passer-by and asked for directions, and was given them with enthusiasm.

'You British?' the native asked pleasantly.

'No, English,' Annie said. The passer-by looked puzzled, smiled uncertainly, and passed on.

'You're incorrigible. Come on,' Ted said, and grabbed her hand to tow her along as if she might at any moment do something unspeakable on the Broadway sidewalk.

Zabars was full of the most wonderful smells. Annie loved delicatessens anyway, and this one was stuffed full of garlic sausages, pâtés, different kinds of breads, cheeses, coffees, and all sorts of things that smelled like heaven. Annie's nerve failed her at the lost moment and she let Ted order for her, listening as if to a magic spell to the words 'Hot pastrami on rye and a sour pickle to go.' Except for the sheer size of everything, it was rather like ordering a hot salt-beef sandwich to take away from Phil Rabins at Piccadilly Circus. Both the sandwich and the coffee were delicious.

'All right, where do you want to go?' Ted asked when they had finished. Annie licked her fingers.

'Mm. I can see Sinatra's point all right. What –? Oh yes, well, what about Greenwich Village?'

'Why?'

'*I* don't know. Just the name, I suppose. I like our Greenwich.'

'It isn't the same. Anyway, it's on the other side of town. Can't you think of anywhere this side you want to see?'

'How do I know what I want to see? I've never been here before,' Annie said reasonably. 'The only thing I can think of is Greenwich Village.'

'All right then, we'll take a bus.'

'Whee! Thank heaven you're with me. I'd never have the nerve to get on public transport in a foreign city. I once got on a *Strassenbahn* in Düsseldorf and couldn't work out how to get off. I went on and on – it was terrifying. When I got to the terminus I had to take a taxi back, and it cost me a fortune.'

They took the bus, Ted managing everything with a cosmopolitan ease that made Annie seriously admire him, and she teased him about it to cover up her genuine admiration. He looked terribly English, she thought, next to the native New Yorkers. It was funny how, even if you disregarded the different clothes and accents, you could still spot an English person in New York, just as you could spot an American in London. Their faces were different. Ted, with his straight, soft, toffee-coloured hair, innocent brown eyes and smooth, fine face, couldn't have been anything but English, dress him how you liked.

Greenwich Village turned out to be not at all like her imaginings. She had told herself that it wasn't really a village, but could not help being disappointed all the same when it was not even as much of a village as Chelsea, whose King's Road it resembled a little in its remorseless trendiness. Clothes, pottery, leather goods, antiques, 'hand-made crafts' filled the shops, and the prices made Annie gasp when she got round to translating them. One thing they did buy, however, was an ice-cream, and it was out of this world.

'*Real* ice-cream,' Annie said. 'Not like that so-called American muck they sell in London, that tastes as if it's made from reconstituted cardboard. I could never understand why American ice-cream was supposed to be so good, until now.'

'Right little convert you're turning out to be. Have you seen enough? Because we ought to be getting back, if we're going to have something to eat before the concert. And I need a bath, too. We'll get a taxi – enough is enough for one day.'

They ate in the hotel, and after the sandwich and the ice-cream Annie found the food a great disappointment. It looked very nice on the plate, prettily arranged, nice colours, lots of different ingredients, but when she came to eat it, it didn't taste of anything. Not that it tasted bad – it simply tasted of nothing at all. She tried closing her eyes, and apart from the different textures, she couldn't have told the meat from the veg in her mouth.

'Well at least you know it's germ-free,' Ted said when she complained.


The concert was given at the old Philharmonic Hall, which had been renamed Avery Fisher Hall, for reasons that Annie never discovered. The hall staff were very nice to her, and seemed to think it was strange and exciting for her, a woman, to be doing the job she was doing. She tried to point out that it was even more exciting to be one of the seven women musicians (two more had been recruited since she started with the Met Symf) but they shrugged that off as normal. Women had played in orchestras for years, but to be one of the admin staff seemed to them to be rare and wonderful. She gave up.

They played, she thought, wonderfully, and she was terribly proud to be part of them, however minor. They did Tchaikovsky's Fifth Symphony, and when it came to the horn solo in the second movement, her eyes were naturally drawn to Geoffrey. He played it beautifully – he had always had the power to bring tears to her eyes with his playing, but now especially she found herself moved; she thought of the days when she had stood in front of such an orchestra, part of the music, not just an onlooker; she thought of the love she had had with him, and the love she had thought she had; of her baby, long lost to her, along with her career and everything she valued. And, when the tears were running freely down her face, she thought, too, of Angus, and that finished her, and she had to go to the ladies' to get it all out, and recover herself, and mop up.

After the concert there was a party held by one of the leading New York hostesses in her apartment for the orchestra and select members of the city's society. Annie, on her way there, wondered how on earth everyone could be expected to fit in, but she discovered that *apartment* doesn't mean at all the same thing as *flat*, at least, not in the circles in which their hostess moved. Annie was stunned by so much wealth. The rooms were huge, the carpets so thick you almost had to wade through them, the furniture new and expensive, the drinks plentiful and served by uniformed maids. There was cold cocktail food laid out, and that was pretty to look at, but again curiously tasteless, except the caviar which tasted salty. One wall of one room was entirely made of huge glass doors which opened on to a patio-garden, with a fountain and potted shrubs and a view over Central Park. Annie was standing by the parapet looking out when an arm came round her waist, and she knew from the smell of his aftershave that it was Geoffrey.

'Hello,' he said. 'Don't jump – aren't you enjoying yourself?'

'Oh yes,' she said. She turned to look up at him, and he drew her closer against his warmth.

'Liar,' he said gently. 'What's the matter? You've been crying.'

'You know me too well,' she said. 'I'm in a melancholy sort of mood. It was your solo brought it on.'

'*I* made you cry?' he asked, as if flattered.

'You often did,' she said. He looked serious. His fingers were almost biting into her bare shoulder. 'It's all right,' she said. 'I've no recriminations.'

'I have,' he said. There was a silence, and they each sipped their drink to pass over the awkwardness. 'What's with you and that trumpeter?' he asked suddenly.

'Why do you ask?' she countered. He looked at her searchingly. 'I don't have to answer,' she added.

'No, you don't.' He feigned indifference, and then laughed. 'You shouldn't get yourself mixed up with trumpeters. Inferior brass.'

'He used to play the horn,' she said, remembering it suddenly. 'Until someone revealed to him that the trumpet was really the queen of instruments.'

'I'll bet it was a woman,' Geoffrey said savagely. Annie laughed.

'Right first time. Why?'

'They can never resist the earthy approach.'

'It was him that couldn't resist her, I believe, not vice versa.'

'You know a lot about him,' Geoffrey said.

'Objections?'

He used the leverage of her shoulder to turn her towards him. She was now much too close to him for her own sanity. He was holding her by both her shoulders, and his face was only inches from hers, lit while hers was in shadow. 'Oh Annie,' he said, and his hands slid round her back.

'Please don't,' she said helplessly. 'Please don't.' But he did. Remorselessly he drew her to him, and then they were kissing. Oh God, his mouth, the shape and taste of him, so familiar, so lovely, it was like coming home. The smell of his skin, the taste of his tongue in her mouth, the shape of his lips and strong, even teeth to her tongue-tip, his hard shoulders under her hands, the springy silk of his hair, the feeling of his hands on her skin, demanding. She was melting inside, turning to warm flowing water, flowing with desire for him, wanting to be closer and closer to him, to be inside and outside and all around him, to *be* him.

He dragged his mouth away from hers and pressed it to her ear, muffled by her hair. 'Let's skip this party, shall we? Let's go?'

Weak, foolish, stupid, weak, she nodded. She felt herself nod, allowed her hand to slip into his, allowed him to pilot them safely and unseen through the crowded rooms, down in the elevator, and into a waiting taxi. The journey was not long, and they did not speak, but their hands were never still, touching, turning, caressing, their breathing rapid and shallow as if they were fever victims. At the hotel Geoffrey paid the taxi-driver, and he watched them go in his mirror, a cynical smile turning his lips, for he had seen it all before.

Annie was no longer fully conscious of her surroundings. She was in a daze of love and anxiety, anxiety dimmed and made hazy by the force of her love and desire, thwarted and bottled up all these years. She went with him like an automaton, dumb and obedient, letting him guide her, letting him take the responsibility for what was going to happen. In his room, the door locked with the DO NOT DISTURB notice hung outside, they turned to each other at last. The dim light from the curtained window was enough – they didn't need more. They knew each other, despite the intervening years, as well as they knew their own bodies.

Annie's dress had one zip, and under it she wore only pants. When she was naked, his hands shook so much that he was slow and clumsy with all his more elaborate clothing. Clad only in her pale-honey hair, she helped him. She knew evening wear of old. Cummerbund and tie, dress-shirt and trousers were no mysteries to her. She undressed him like a child, while his otherwise helpless hands stroked and explored her, remembering.

Now they were naked, and as one they lay down upon the bed, and he paused a moment, troubled, wondering if he was being too precipitate. She pulled at him.

'No, please, don't wait. Not this time.'

With a groan of thankfulness he lay down and eased into her, and they both gave an involuntary sigh of accomplished desire to be home again, together again after so long. They clung to each other, raining kisses on every surface of each other's bodies that was near enough, clutching with their hands like drowning mariners. There was no thought, no conscious design; they moved involuntarily, in the grip of something beyond them both, their minds empty of everything but pleasure. At the last moment, Annie gave a little cry like someone tortured beyond bearing, and he cried out to her, *Annie!*, as if she was being taken away from him. And then they were *there*, together, as one, at last.

Some time afterwards they were still lying together on the top of his bed. Annie's head was on his chest, and his hand was folding again and again through her silky hair. They were silent, each engaged with thoughts they did not yet want to share. At last she sighed and lifted her head a little and said, 'I'm hungry.'

'Do you want to go out?' he asked. He unwrapped his hand, releasing her.

'Not particularly. Can you have food sent up here?'

'If it isn't too exotic. What do you want?'

'A steak sandwich,' she decided. He ordered the same for himself, and coffee and whisky. When the knock on the door came, she went into the bathroom, and when Geoffrey called the all-clear, she came out again, washed and refreshed and sat cross-legged on the bed beside him while they ate and drank.

'I must go back after this,' she said at last. He raised an eyebrow.

'*Must* you?' She nodded. 'Back to what? Or to whom? That trumpeter of yours?'

'Are you jealous of him?' she asked, suddenly enlightened. He smiled coolly.

'My dear girl, you're a grown woman. You do as you please. As I do.'

She avoided this thought. 'I meant, I must go back to my room.' He did not ask her why, and she was almost disappointed. But he had never tried to tie her to him with any kind of binding.

'I'll see you to your door,' he said courteously. 'And tomorrow, after rehearsal, I'll take you to lunch at the World Trade Center. You ought to see *that* at least before you leave New York.' He knew, of course, that she had never been here before. He knew, somehow, everything about her. 'There's a restaurant there called Windows on the World.'

'Is that the famous one? I was told it was impossible to get a table there.'

'Not at lunch-time. At night, you have to book a long way ahead, or you have to have influence. I could get a table. Would you like to eat there one evening?'

'Yes,' she said. 'But I haven't any grand clothes. Only working-clothes.'

'We can buy you something. New York, in case you hadn't noticed, is full of shops. I'll tell you what, we'll go shopping tomorrow afternoon, instead of going to the Center, and

93

then we'll have dinner after the concert and you can be stunned by the night view instead of the day view. All right?'

'It sounds lovely.' As it had always been with Geoffrey, he did the organising. It came naturally to him, and it came naturally to her to let him, just as when she was with Ted it was she who would organise.

A little while later they went down in the lift together to the tenth floor where her room was, silent but in accord. He stood very close to her, his hand on her shoulder, wound in her hair.

'That's it, the door opposite,' she said as they stepped out. He stood by the lift door, holding it open, while he watched her get out her key and let herself in. Then he said, 'Good night, Annie. Sleep well.'

'Good night,' she said. She watched him turn and step into the lift, and all the questions she had forced herself not to ask welled up in her. There was so much she wanted to know.

'How is Sacha?' the words burst out of her. But it was too late. The lift doors were already closing, and he did not hear her.

She dreamt a strange and puzzling dream that night in which she danced the whole of Swan Lake in a private performance in somebody's flat to an audience that contained Geoffrey and Angus and last night's abandoned hostess, but she woke feeling refreshed, and her first thoughts on waking were of Geoffrey, and how marvellous it was to be in love again, in spite of everything.

'And a hell of an everything that's going to be,' she muttered to herself as she went down to breakfast. She decided to try blueberry pancakes with a side order of bacon – after all, when in Rome, never let a dago by, and all that sort of thing. The pancakes were delicious but very filling, and she was reluctantly abandoning the last of the heap when Ted came down, looking rather bleary-eyed.

'Hello – what happened to you last night?' he asked.

'I don't need to ask what happened to you,' she said. 'I can see it in your veins. Whooping it up all night, eh?'

'It's these American drinks,' he said. 'Twice as much alcohol in them as the European equivalent. I was pee'd before I knew it. Mind you, so was everyone else. Paddy Cramer was dancing an Irish jig on the rim of the fountain, accompanied on the spoons by David.'

'Don't tell me – he fell in?'

'He was pushed in,' Ted corrected. 'His balance seemed unimpaired, and, well, what would a party be without someone falling in something? So – someone – gave him a little nudge and –splot! Instant success.'

'Someone being you, I take it.'

'Well,' he smirked modestly. 'Willment Contractors, Party Organisers,' he announced. 'Make Your Party Go with a Swing. Ideas to suit all pockets.'

'Have some black coffee,' she suggested. 'You're going to need it.' And at that moment Geoffrey came through the swing doors, looked around, smiled and nodded a good morning to her, and took himself off to a table on his own.

Ted looked from Geoffrey to Annie, and then picked up his menu and began to study it. He did not ask any more questions – he didn't need to. When he had ordered coffee and scrambled eggs, he said to Annie, 'Where do you want to go sightseeing today?' She coloured slightly.

'Oh – I – er – I've already made an arrangement for lunch. I'm sorry,' Annie said. Ted smiled, looking into her eyes with a frank and kindly look.

'That's all right. Not to worry,' he said. She was grateful to him for taking it that way. He could have embarrassed her, and many men would have, if only to save face. But Ted went on talking about something else in a perfectly normal and friendly manner, and she could have blessed him. Never had she appreciated so much what a nice person he really was.

95

# EIGHT

Shopping was done in Saks in Fifth Avenue, and the prices made Annie blink and swallow nervously. She had mentally equated Fifth Avenue with Oxford Street, and it wasn't a bit the same. She tried on one or two things, and Geoffrey told her she must have the Saint-Laurent dress which had a gold lamé top and a wide velvet skirt in a deep golden-brown colour.

'Only blondes can wear yellow successfully,' Geoffrey said, 'and even then, only natural blondes.' When it came to the question of money, he drew out his wallet unconcernedly, and Annie felt she had to protest.

'Why?' he said. 'The money makes no difference to me, and it wouldn't be the first time you've accepted a present from me, so why baulk at this? Did you intend to pay for your own dinner tonight?'

'No, of course not, but –' she began. He grinned suddenly.

'I like the "of course not". Pay for the dress yourself if you like, darling, or let me pay – it really makes no difference at all.'

Of course, she couldn't buy a dress that cost as much as that, and, not liking to seem ungracious, she let him pay without arguing any further. After that he called a taxi and they drove across town to lunch at the Fraunces Tavern, which, he told her, was famous for being Terribly Old and Quaint. The food turned out to be very good, but Annie could not be impressed with the architecture – the place had been so thoroughly renovated and decorated that she said it reminded her of Arterial Road Tudor.

'Perhaps it's a mistake to bring an English person to an old place in America – one should stick to admiring the new, which they do so well,' Geoffrey said. 'The Americans themselves love this place, but I suppose when one rubs shoulders with Hever Castle and Hampton Court and

Salisbury Cathedral, it's hard to be impressed with a place like this.'

After lunch Geoffrey obliged by telling the taxi-driver to take them round some of the sights, and he himself gave Annie a running commentary on what they saw. It was so different, she thought guiltily, being shown around by someone like Geoffrey, who knew the place and didn't mind spending money, from being shown it by someone like Ted. At five he took her into a café called Chocfulonuts, where some of the doughnuts were, and fed her on coffee and cakes 'so that you don't starve to death during the concert', and then dropped her off at the hotel saying that he had business to attend to. Annie went up to her room, clutching her prestigious Saks carrier bag, to shower and rest on her bed until it was time to get dressed for the evening. She would, of course, have to go to the hall in her black, and take the Saint-Laurent to change into there.

It was perhaps unfortunate that the programme that evening included Schubert's Unfinished Symphony, because it put Annie in a sentimental mood before she even got to the romantic scene of dinner. She and Geoffrey had particular memories of the Unfinished, for it had been played on the evening that they first went out together, and went to bed together. Geoffrey had joked tenderly at the time that the theme in the first movement was a song from him to her, with the words "Annie, make love to me,' and now as she stood in the wings listening to the Met Symf the words ran through her head every time the theme arose.

When the last movement of the last piece started she went into the women's dressing-room to change and do her face, so that she would be ready when the orchestra came off the platform, for all Geoffrey had to do was to change his tail-coat for a dinner-jacket, the dress trousers being equal to both. Doing her face and hair was a simple task, for hers were the kind of looks that depended on good bones. Much make-up only detracted from her wide grey eyes, and her straight pale hair was very well cut in a simple style that virtually nothing could alter. After some thought, she dabbed on Givenchy's L'interdit, thinking it would perhaps be playing too much on memory's nerves to wear the usual Balenciaga.

She came out of the dressing-room in time to hear the applause, and slipped to the exit curtain to take a look. The audience was on its feet, but it wasn't what you could call a standing ovation in European terms, since American audiences always seemed to stand up, however good or bad the performance, just out of sheer politeness. She backed off as the players came streaming off and past her. Some of them whistled or made remarks on her appearance – there was no mistaking how expensive the dress was, even to those who knew nothing of *haute couture* – but Ted merely nodded to her, almost without a smile. She was sorry, very sorry, that she should be the cause of hurting him, if his behaviour *was* indicative of hurt, but nothing had ever been said between them that committed one to the other, so she was not in the least guilty.

Geoffrey was in and out of the dressing-room in a flash, and before the backstage area had even begun to clear he was helping Annie into a taxi and following her in with his instrument case in his hand.

'It's like taking a child everywhere with you,' she complained as it got between them somehow and dug into her hip. 'Always in the way.'

'You shouldn't go out with musicians, then,' Geoffrey said with a smile. 'Just be thankful I don't play the double-bass.'

The World Trade Center building was very impressive. 'I'm impressed at last,' Annie told Geoffrey, staring up at some of it. 'It's against nature, though, like jumbo jets. I can't see any reason why it should stay up there.'

'You wait until you get up to the hundredth floor. The tower sways so far to either side you can *feel* it. Like those silent films where someone's up a ladder and it comes away from the wall.'

99

'I'm glad you told me,' she said. And he was right – she could feel it. 'And to think I avoided going up the Post Office Tower,' she said. After the huge entrance hall, all white marble and oval windows, like something out of a space-movie, she had wondered how much more impressed she could be, but when they were shown to their table beside the huge thick glass windows, she had no words for her feelings. The city was a quarter of a mile below them, and spread away in a million fiery jewels for miles and miles and miles. It was some time before she could drag her eyes away to consult the menu, but the waiters were used to that and didn't hurry them.

'Thank you,' she said at last to Geoffrey. 'It's an experience of a lifetime just being here.'

'With me?' Geoffrey said. 'Yes, of course. And the view isn't bad either, is it?' But even his joking couldn't alter the wonder of the moment for her. When they had ordered and were sitting in silence, staring out of the window, the waiter came back to show a couple to the next table. It was Warren Stacker accompanied by a young woman wearing real diamonds. He smiled at them and gave a little wave of the hand, which Geoffrey returned. The woman ignored them.

'Can't get away from them,' Annie said. 'So much for it being impossible to get a table here.'

Geoffrey laughed at her. 'You *are* an innocent,' he said. 'It's she who has brought *him*. I don't think it can be very difficult to get a table when your name's Stuyvesant.'

'Oh,' said Annie, taking another look. 'I wish you wouldn't tell me these things. I'm feeling nervous now.'

'Don't be. You are the most beautiful woman in this room, and beauty is sufficient entry to *this* world. Not all their money can buy it.'

Annie drew breath to stop her voice trembling, and said, 'Strange that it should have been the "Unfinished" tonight.' He looked at her oddly, and she was suddenly afraid that he had forgotten.

'Not strange,' he said. 'But appropriate, nevertheless. We have a little unfinished business between us, don't we, *Anna*

*Dushka?*' His eyes looking into hers were such an intimate caress that it made her go hot and weak.

'I feel a bit guilty,' she said.

'Why? Because of Shona? You shouldn't.' he said. 'We have an arrangement, she and I. You must have worked it out for yourself, child – you know that she's paralysed. You surely mustn't have thought she'd expect me to be a monk for the rest of my life.'

'But she must *mind*, however reasonable she is about it,' Annie said. He shrugged. 'She must, in all reason.'

'Perhaps,' he said. 'But that isn't your concern. What happens between you and me is between you and me, and not the concern of anyone else.'

Fool rush in. 'Not necessarily. One thing that happened between you and me is very much her concern.'

His face closed, his eyes became cold. 'I don't want to talk about that,' he said.

'But I do,' she rushed on, stopping abruptly as the waiter came with their first course. When he had gone again Geoffrey tried to change the subject, but she would not let him.

'I hope you like this. It's a speciality –'

'Geoffrey, I want to talk about him. I want to know about him.'

'About my son?' he said carefully. He looked at her as if she were a stranger, almost with hatred.

'My son too!' she said passionately.

'I'm afraid not. You gave up all right to that title. You chose your career.'

Anger rushed through her like bile, anger and shame and indignation.

'*You* never had to make that choice! That was the only difference. You could get away with it, being a man. You ended up with everything, and I ended up with nothing. Does that give you the right to criticise me? What would you have done in my place?'

'I don't know,' he said harshly. 'I only know *I* wouldn't have betrayed *you* so easily.'

101

She was speechless, tears rising to her eyes with involuntary ease as she stared at him. He made a gesture with his hand as though he had been going to reach out and touch her, and changed his mind.

'Eat your food,' he said. 'This isn't the time or place. And please don't cry, this isn't Lyon's Corner House.'

She swallowed everything, sorrow and anger, and applied herself to her food, forcing it past the lump in her throat like shoving bricks into a sack. It had no taste, though she would never know if that was because of her feelings or because of the usual American hygiene. When the waiter came to remove their plates and bring the next course, Geoffrey applied himself to social chit-chat, and made a sufficiently cheerful noise to pass over the moment, and give her time to recover herself. Moments later Warren came across in the pause between *his* courses, and leaned his fists on the table between them, breathing the sweet reek of expensive cocktails over them.

'Hello,' he said. 'Fancy seeing you here. I didn't know you knew each other – or are you just a fast worker, Annie?'

'We've known each other for some time,' Geoffrey said calmly. 'I'm more surprised to see you here – I didn't know you had such influence.'

'Not influence,' Warren said, slightly slurred. 'Friend of a friend of someone I met when I lived here introduced me. Fact is, I've been "taken up" by Bunny. No objection really – she pays for everything. That sort of thing's all right here. Especially as I'm a penniless artist – it counts as patronising the arts. Though between you and me, it's more a case of me patronising the arse –'

'Yes, well, no more of that,' Geoffrey said hastily. 'Hadn't you better get back to your table?'

'Oh yes, I'd better at that – she's giving me funny looks, seeing me talking to another woman. Of course, you arrange things better, don't you Geoff, old boy – one in the afternoon, and one in the evening. This afternoon's one looked richer, but I like our homegrown products better,' he said, giving Annie's shoulder a pat. 'Any time you feel like leaving the wind sections for the strings, Annie-old-thing, let me know.'

And with that he pushed himself off his hands and sauntered back to his own table.

'What was all that about?' Annie asked. Geoffrey raised an eyebrow.

'Only his way of insulting each of us,' he said. 'Or, if you mean the bit about this afternoon's one being richer, I was having coffee with a lady in the hotel coffee-shop when Warren came in.'

'Oh,' Annie said. There was a moment's silence as she absorbed the fact that he was not going to tell her who it was, and he absorbed the fact that she wasn't going to ask him. It wasn't her business. She had no doubt he was starting two hares at once, but that had always been his way. He wasn't likely to change now.

After their dinner, he took her to the building's observation deck on the hundred-and-tenth floor. It was like the restaurant view, only more so, and it was chilly so he slipped off his jacket and hung it over her shoulders. She didn't object, especially since he followed it up by putting his arms around her shoulders and drawing her against him. She loved to be touching him – it was like relief from an intolerable ache.

After a moment, he hummed the theme from the 'Unfinished', and she realised it had been running through her head too. In the old days, their thoughts had often kept pace, and they would both start to say the same thing at the same time.

'To me,' he said softly, 'it was saying "Annie, come back to me".'

She said nothing for a long time, and then she turned her head to look up at him searchingly.

'I wish I knew how much you meant by that. If it was anyone else, it would be clear and simple. But with you – there's Shona, and Sacha, and all those other ladies, afternoon and otherwise.'

'You know the way I am – why try to change me now?'

'I wouldn't. I wouldn't want to change you. I think that's what tells you the difference between real love and anything else – when you love someone, you don't want to change them. But you know that I'm not like that – not like you. I don't think it would be enough for me.'

'It used to be,' he said.

'I was younger then. I was young, and I had so much. I had – music. I had music then.'

He pressed her against him in mute sympathy. 'Maybe it will come back,' he said. She shook her head. 'Not now. Not after – Sacha,' she said.

There was a silence, then, 'He's a wonderful boy. He looks so much like you. People say he looks like me, and when I look at him – well, I've wondered sometimes if you and I look alike? Strange thought.'

'Does he know about me?'

'That you exist. Not who you are.'

'Shona must –'

'Things have changed a lot,' he broke in, speaking hurriedly as if afraid of losing his nerve before things were said. 'He's at school now, and of course he has a nannie. And then Shona has a sort of nurse-companion, and she's often away – she needs the sun a lot, to keep the rheumatism at bay. I think sometimes that really, there's nothing keeping us together – the three of us – no nucleus –'

'The three of you,' she said painfully. He turned her round, holding her by the shoulders so that he could look into her face.

'Annie, I've sometimes wondered – recently – why it was that we did what we did. Sometimes it seems ludicrous to me that you and I didn't marry instead – it would have been so much simpler. Of course, there was Shona, but she could hardly have expected I would stay with her. Why didn't I leave her and marry you? It must have been because you wanted your career. You rejected the idea – you abandoned the child –'

'It would make it simpler for you to believe that, wouldn't it?' she said. 'But if I said now, all right, I'll come back to you,

104

what would you do then? What would you tell the child? Have you thought of that?' He evidently hadn't. She saw him thinking it out. 'What would you tell Shona? Look, I've had plenty of time to think about it, over these past years. I *know* you, I know why you did what you did. Shona gives you your freedom, that's why you wouldn't part from her. She's your excuse. If you weren't married to her, you'd have to marry someone who wouldn't let you be a bachelor and screw around and do what you want. She can't object to you being unfaithful, and she can't have more children to tie you down, and no one else you get involved with can demand marriage of you, because you're married already, and people say "What a wonderful man he must be, to stick by his crippled wife like that". So it's no good pretending with me, Geoffrey. I know the truth about you.' She paused for breath, and he did not speak, having nothing to say. She finished in a lower voice. 'What I don't know is the truth about myself.'

'We'd better go back,' he said. 'You're beginning to shiver.' She was, but it wasn't entirely the cold.

They drove back to the hotel in silence, though not a hostile silence. In the lift they found themselves alone, and so he began to kiss her, his hands going automatically, without even thought, to the zip of her dress, and she thrust her hands inside his jacket, liking to feel his flesh so close, only a shirt's thickness away. But when she got to the door of his room, she baulked, like a spooked horse.

'What's the matter?' he asked, and then, exasperated, 'Why the hell not? What difference does it make?'

'It makes a difference to me. I don't think I can take it, Geoffrey, not the way it is.'

'What do you want, then?'

'Look,' she said desperately, 'I love you, I love you more than I can bear, and I'd come back to you like a shot, at the drop of a coin, but I can't see any way it can possibly be done.'

'Annie –'

'No, no, please let me go. Geoffrey –'

He let go of her, and stared at her blackly, bitterly. 'Go on, then.'

'Please –' she began, but he turned away from her harshly.

'Go on, go, now you've got what you wanted. What are you waiting for?' She shrugged, and walked away, and he called after her softly, 'You'll regret it. I'll make you regret it.'

She ran, as if the lift were a sanctuary, and managed to hold off the tears until she reached the haven of her room and locked the door between her and the world.


There was no rehearsal the next morning, and everyone was late up and late to breakfast. Annie sat alone, miserably fiddling with a bowl of grapefruit segments, and Ted came and joined her, miraculously divining that she wanted him there, God knows how.

'Don't be miserable,' he said. 'Nothing's worth it.'

'I'm coming to that conclusion myself,' she said, looking up and trying to smile.

'Oh?' He tried to look interested without looking too interested, and at the sight of his struggle her half-smile reached maturity. Encouraged, he said, 'Bad words between you?'

'Words don't hurt,' she said obliquely. 'I'm safe now, but I'm afraid my resolution won't last. I can resist anything but temptation.'

'Put yourself out of temptation's way, then,' he said.

'What do you suggest.'

'Spend more time with me. Spend all your time with me.'

'You mean go out sightseeing or something?'

'I was thinking rather longer-term than that,' he said diffidently. 'I could protect you from yourself much better if you were to marry me.'

Having said it, he seemed to hold his breath. She stared at him, amazed, a proposal being the last thing she would have expected. He pursued crumbs around the table-cloth, giving her a view of the top of his head only.

'You aren't joking?' she hazarded. Then he looked up, and she saw the naked emotion in his face that he had been trying, out of politeness, to hide from her.

'I'm not joking,' he said softly.

'Oh,' she said. She hunted around for words to refuse him without hurting him, and he went on, 'Don't refuse right away – I'm in no hurry for an answer. At least think about it. It has its advantages. I think you could do with being loved a little. We're good company, we're great in bed, we have lots of interests in common. And it would stop you doing anything foolish with him.'

'Would it? I'm not sure.'

'All right, it might not absolutely stop you, but it would give you an incentive not to. You might even find after a while that you didn't want to.'

'So modest,' she said. 'You don't value yourself highly enough. Why should you want second-best with me, when you could have someone who loved you as you deserve?'

'Because it's you I want.'

'On any terms?'

'On any terms.'

She considered. 'I don't think I like that. You shouldn't have to accept something on any terms.'

'Well, that proves you love me a little,' he said, smiling a little painfully.

'Oh darling, I love you a lot,' she said. 'But you know, don't you, that I love Geoffrey. He comes first with me. I couldn't love you that way.'

'I know. It doesn't matter.'

'Perhaps it does to me. Sex with you is marvellous, and I love being with you, but –'

'What else is there?' he asked. 'That sounds like everything.'

'Is it, though? If I have a loyalty that comes before you –'

'I'm willing to take that risk. I have confidence in us. I think, after a while, those feelings would go away. I think you need me. Think about it.'

They spent the day together, not speaking of that or of

Geoffrey or of their feelings – a day almost like the times they had spent before the troubles began, when Angus so often made a happy third with them. They took a boat trip up the Hudson River, and when they had disembarked walked aimlessly through one of the riverside parks, talking nonsense, hardly aware of their surroundings, until it was time to go back and change for the concert.

While they played she watched them, trying to sort out her feelings. What she had said to Geoffrey hadn't changed, and yet it was so wonderful just to see him, just to be near him. When they went back to England and he went back to his orchestra, would she have the strength of mind not to miss him so much that she went rushing after him? Wouldn't the longing grow so strong again that nothing but going back to him would assuage it?

And Ted, sitting there at the back, neat and clean and very, very English – what did she feel about him? She liked him very much, but was it enough? She was afraid she would want to change him, as she had seen happen to other couples who didn't love each other enough; and if she did, either he would resist and they would quarrel, or he would give in and she would despise him.

On the other hand, she thought suddenly, could she bear to give him up entirely? She looked at him, looked at his hands and mouth and strong neck, his dark, warm, fathomless eyes, and she shivered. Suppose, now, suppose you were told you'd never see him again? Yes, that would shake you, wouldn't it? She felt weak and lonely and needy. Perhaps – perhaps she would just let him persuade her, and then if anything happened it would be his fault. Coward, she derided herself, but with an inner laugh. It was the kind of reasoning she would have expected of Geoffrey.

When the concert was over, she waited for Ted, and took his arm and said, 'I don't know about you, but I feel like an early night.'

He looked at her quickly to read her intent, and then said, 'I always feel like an early night.' And he let his hand brush against her breast, and she shivered again.

'Let's hurry back,' she murmured. 'I want you *now*.'

It was as marvellous as before, though she thought now that she had the clue to it – it was because he was in love with her. His excitement excited her. Or perhaps it was just that he had more than his fair share of sexual attraction. Why should she be so lucky as to be the one he wanted? While he lay, face down beside her as usual, to get his breath back, she looked him over, admiring and desiring all over again, and rolled over to stroke his shoulders and the deep cleft at his waist. He turned his head slightly, and one brown eye regarded her expressionlessly. She put her mouth to his ear, bit the rim, dug her tongue into its convolutions. He groaned and rolled over, catching hold of her, grabbing her head in his two hands to hold her still.

'Want me again,' she said, and he was not sure if it was a demand or a question. She bared her teeth at him, pushing her body hard against him. 'Make me want you. God, you're lovely!'

Panting, he rolled her on to her back, slid over on top of her. She hung on to him as if she were suspended above a great height. She was torn in two, her body wanting and needing and reacting to him, her mind suffering. She hid her face in his hair while he loved her, but when she closed her eyes at the moment of climax, it was him she saw against the closed lids, not Geoffrey. At last there was no thought in her head but him.

'I will marry you,' she said afterwards as they were drifting into sleep, his head in the hollow of her shoulder, cradled like a child's. He murmured sleepily, but she wasn't sure he had heard her. Never mind, she thought, hugging him. She would tell him again in the morning. She was sure now.

Almost sure.

# NINE

The feeling of sureness seemed to exist only when she was alone with him, particularly in bed. When they were out and about and in the presence of other people, she found herself growing more doubtful. It was as if the fabric of her was stretched and thinned the longer she was out of his arms. It worried her considerably, the more so because he obviously had no doubts, was so happy it radiated off him like a saint's aura.

Tam, the Scots roadie, noticed it at once and said to Annie as he strode past her with a double-bass.

'Hey, what's wi' oor Ted the day? He's like a dog wi' two tails. Huv you finally said yes tae the poor bugger?'

'Said yes to what?' Annie said. Tam grinned lasciviously.

'Ye ken fine what,' he said. 'I've seen the way he looks at you. He's been pantin' for ye ever since the first day you came, hen.'

'You noticed more than I did, I must say. I thought that was just the way all the lads looked at women.'

Tam considered this. 'Aye, well, they all fancied you, o' course, but wi' him it was a bit mair than that. Did he ask you tae marry him yet?'

'You really do ask the questions, don't you,' Annie said, blushing. Tam narrowed his eyes.

'You've said yes, then,' he concluded. 'That'll mean you'll be leavin', and we'll have tae get used tae anither OA. Benny'll no be pleased.'

'But why? I hadn't thought of leaving,' Annie said, puzzled.

'Ye'll leave,' Tam prophesied. 'Ye've no thought what it wud be like, livin' an' workin' all day long wi' the same bloke. Aye, ye'll leave a' right.'

Later the same day David Bastowe said to Annie, 'Here, what have you done to poor old Ted? He nearly blew his brains out this morning – took the valves out of his horn to clean them, and put them in back to front.'

'Why should I be responsible for his lack of concentration?' Annie protested. David shrugged.

'I don't know why. The rest of us have managed to get used to the sight of you prancing about half-naked, but it seems to get him worse than anybody else. Anyway, lay off him a bit, will you? It's hard enough playing second to him at the best of times, but at the moment – well, I think he thinks that trumpet of his came with a pair of wings and a halo.'

Annie asked Ted to keep the news of their marriage secret for the time being, and he agreed with a shrug, though she had a nasty feeling that he thought she wanted it secret because she wasn't sure if she might not yet back out of it. Even worse, she had the feeling he was right.

'All the same,' he said, 'for the cure to work, there's one person who ought to be told, isn't there?'

'Geoffrey, you mean?' she said. She hesitated. He was right, and yet the last person she wanted to know it was Geoffrey. It would be, wouldn't it, another betrayal? Ted watched her understandingly.

'I'll tell him for you, if you like,' he said. She squared her shoulders.

'No, no – I'll do it. You're right. I'll tell him as soon as I see him.'

'Well, now's your chance – here he comes. I'll make myself scarce.' And very honourably, he left her to it. Geoffrey slowed as he saw the manoeuvre, and came up to Annie's side with curiosity.

'What's all that about?' he asked. 'One presumes from the look of addled bliss on his face all morning that you slept with him last night – but why is he trotting off so obediently to leave the field free for me?' Annie did not immediately answer – she was trying to frame the words in her head. He went on musingly, 'Now I wonder whether it betokens so much confidence that he isn't worried about leaving you alone with me, or so little that he knows there is no point in resisting the inevitable?'

Annie met his eye, and feeling her courage draining away she blurted out, 'Geoffrey, I'm going to marry him.'

There was a silence as Geoffrey's eye searched hers for the truth, and then, shatteringly, he burst out laughing.

'Marry Ted? That's a good one! No, you'll have to try harder than that, my darling! Much harder.'

'It's true!' Annie said angrily. He continued to laugh, shaking his head.

'No, no,' he said at last, 'it won't do. You may think you're going to just at the moment, but you won't do it. Marry Ted! You wouldn't go through with it, believe me.'

'We'll see,' she said, still angrily, and turned away. He let her go only one step before he caught her arm and stopped her. She kept her face turned away from him, but she couldn't stop herself hearing the quiet words.

'You won't do it. You're mine, you know. You always have been. And I've a fancy to have you back.'

She shook herself free and went on.

The rest of the New York stay passed without incident. Geoffrey made no attempts on her, which was just as well, considering the state of her mind, for she had enough trouble controlling herself when he even just looked at her. On the other hand, the times she spent alone with Ted were wonderful. His happiness seemed to light up everything around him, made their love-making all the more wonderful, made Annie happy and proud to be the cause of it. She discovered a lot more about him, re-discovered how wide his interests were, how lively his mind, how sound his education. They never could have done talking, for between them they had enough to discuss to last them their lifetimes.

In the aeroplane going home he said to her, 'We can't keep the secret much longer. We'll have to tell the Board and the concerts manager to arrange for the time off. I was thinking we ought to get married in August. We've got three days free then anyway, and if we can get them to replace us for the Edinburgh trip, that will give us two clear weeks. But they'll have to be given reasonable notice.'

That reminded Annie of Tam's words. 'I was wondering

how it will be to work together as well as being married. Won't it be too much?'

He seemed not to have considered this. 'I don't see why,' he said at last. 'I don't think I'd mind spending all my time with you but, in any case, while we're playing we're not actually together. I mean, there I am, up on the platform, and you're elsewhere, pottering about.'

'Mm,' she said uncertainly.

'Besides,' he said, 'look how many Met Symf marriages have broken up because we're hardly ever at home. At least *we* won't have that trouble.'

'Yes,' she said. 'And that brings up another problem – what about home? Where shall we live.'

He smiled at her. 'Why is that a problem? We can live at my house when we're in London. But if you want to keep on your flat, there's no reason why you shouldn't. It might even come in handy, for rushing home for a screw at lunch-time.' This raised a faint smile. 'Why are you searching round for problems, Annie? Have you changed your mind? Don't you want to go on with it?'

'It isn't that,' she said, and then paused. 'It isn't that,' she said again, feebly.

'You don't want it made public?'

'I see that we have to, but – can we wait until we've told my people? Just till then.'

'If you like. Don't worry about it. Everything will be all right.'

Julie was delighted. 'I little thought that evening when we all went to dinner together that it would come to this,' she said. 'I'm very, very happy for you both. When's it going to be? Have you decided?'

'In August,' Ted answered for them both. 'In London. I hope you'll come. I believe Annie wants you as matron-of-honour.'

'Of course we'll come, won't we, Pat? You couldn't keep us away! I'm really really pleased for you both! It couldn't have happened to two nicer people.' And she kissed Ted happily and beamed at Annie. Annie turned more uncertainly to Pat, who had said very little so far.

'Will you give me away, Pat? I haven't anyone else.'

'No, of course you haven't. One thing, Ted, you won't have to worry about in-law trouble. There's only us, and we're pretty human.' He looked sharply at Annie. 'Come with me and let's sort out a bottle of wine to celebrate with,' he said, and obediently she followed him out of the room. There was a kind of cupboard-cum-larder between the kitchen and the back door in which Pat kept his wine, and in the privacy of this small room, with the door pushed discreetly to, he turned on her sternly.

'Now what's all this about?' he asked.

'What's all what about?' she asked feebly. She was forced to meet his eye. 'I thought you liked him. You don't approve, do you?'

'I do like him. I think he'll make a very good husband. He's a nice bloke, and he obviously worships you. But it isn't a matter of whether I approve or not. *You* think you're doing the wrong thing.'

'I don't –' she began to protest. He silenced her with a look.

'I know you,' he said. 'You can't fool me. I suspect you can't fool him either. So why are you doing it?'

'It seemed like an answer. I *do* love him –'

'But not as much as that other bastard.'

'Not the same way. It isn't a matter of more or less – it's just different. Oh, Pat, what should I do? Advise me – I'm so mixed up, *I* don't know what to do.'

'I can't advise you – you must make up your own mind.' Then, seeing her expression, he relented a little, and said, 'If it were me, I'd marry him. He's a really good sort, and marriage isn't all love and starry eyes, you know. Marry him and have some babies and forget all the mess in your past. That would be my advice if I were going to give you any.'

She smiled, and then hugged him, and he held her tight and kissed the top of her head.

115

'Be happy,' he said huskily. 'And if he ever hurts you, tell me, and I'll kill him.'

'He'd never hurt me,' Annie said, muffled by Pat's broad chest. 'I'm only afraid I'll hurt him.'

Meeting Ted's family was much more of an ordeal. He drove her there on a Friday night, for the traditional Sunday Tea First Meeting was impossible for them, since almost every Sunday they worked. 'Relax,' he said, glancing at her sideways as they drove down the M4. 'They'll like you. I hope you like fish, by the way – it's always fish and chips on a Friday.'

'Are they Catholics?' she asked out of a dull agony of doubt and shyness.

'No, just old-fashioned. Cheer up, darling. Smile. You are so beautiful they'll be dazzled, they'll never see past your nimbus.'

She smiled a little stiffly, as if she wasn't used to the exercise. 'I just keep thinking that since you've got to this age without being married, they'll expect you to have chosen something really outstanding.'

'There's no answer to that, is there?' he said lightly, and let his left hand stray across from the gear lever to keep her occupied.

The Willments lived on a raw new housing estate, in a small semi-detached house of clean pink brick and white barge-boarding, with picture windows and a glass front door. Annie knew at once what it would be like inside. Those sorts of mass-produced houses had ceilings so low you felt you had to duck your head when you moved, and a living-room-cum-dining-room with a half-height room divider so that you could never get away from each other, and all the doors would appear to have been made from cardboard. No one, she felt, should have to live in a place like that.

The front garden sported a soldierly display of red salvias, while alyssum and blue lobelia on one side of the path, and on the other a tiny square of very new grass with a standard rose-tree in a circular bed in the centre. The door was opened to them by Mrs Willment, in her best dress with an apron over it. She had evidently had her hair done at the hairdresser's during her lunch hour that day. Mr Willment appeared behind her in the passage, putting his jacket on over his braces. Annie felt sick with fright, and quite desperate.

'Ah, there you are, our Ted. Come in, come in. So this is your young lady is it? Annabel, isn't it? Pleased to meet you, I'm sure.' Mrs Willment ushered them in, and Mr Willment came forward with his hand outstretched.

'How do you do. Nice to see you. Come right in, now, don't be shy. Ted, take your young lady's coat. Come right in here and sit yourself down. Annabel, isn't it? That's a nice old-fashioned name. Mind you, the old names seem to be coming back now, don't they?'

Annie followed him into the sitting-room, resisting the temptation to point out that since she had been given her name quite a long time ago it could hardly be counted as part of a new fashion. The room was exactly as she had expected it. Over the mantelpiece was a reproduction in a silver frame of the Queen's Silver Jubilee photograph. On the wall over the table at the dining-room end of the room was a framed reproduction of Constable's Hay Wain. She sat down on a third of the three-piece suite and tried to smile.

Ted disappeared with his mother, leaving Annie to answer the questions about herself that his father fired at her. Presently other people came in from the kitchen, Ted's brother and sister-in-law, or vice versa, and a sister and brother-in-law, or vice versa, and some offspring of one or other couple, or both, and she was introduced to each one individually, and shook hands, and answered the same questions over again. Her face was stretched into a permanent nervous smile, and she caught one of the sisters looking at the other as if they wondered if she was perhaps an idiot. She couldn't get their names straight, nor their relationships. It was better when they were called to be seated at the table, for then Ted was allowed to sit beside her, and she had something to do to hide the fact that she was totally at a loss.

It wasn't fish and chips, it was tinned salmon and salad, in honour of the occasion, and a large trifle decorated with desiccated coconut and peach slices for dessert, followed by cups of tea and digestive biscuits. Ted was caressing her knee under the table, Mrs Willment and her daughter (in-law?) were discussing their own weddings and making suggestions to Ted as to which was the best photographer to hire, and Mr Willment was telling Annie about his happy years playing the trombone in the works silver band, and asking her yet again if she played anything herself.

'No, I don't play,' she said. She felt as though she was in a dream. She couldn't now remember whether she had answered the question before, or what she had said if she had.

'But I thought you were with the orchestra as well?' he said peevishly. 'Ted said you were. Ted, Ted! I thought you said Arabella was with the orchestra as well?'

'I told you, Dad, she's the OA – that's like the personnel officer. I *told* you that.'

'You never listen, Dad,' said Mavis – or was it Linda? – and went straight on with what she had been saying to Linda (or Mavis). 'The trouble is, as I said, if you have one of the girls as a bridesmaid, you've got to have them all. And to my mind, more than four looks silly, unless you're royalty. I was lucky, really, because there were Claire's two and then your Roy, and the others weren't old enough, and that way I didn't have to worry about cousins and so on – but – are you listening, Ted? I was just saying –'

'But I don't think it will matter with Annabel,' Linda broke in. 'I mean I know what you mean about royalty, but after all she is very good-looking, and she could probably get away with a long train and any number of bridesmaids. It depends what church they're getting married in really. Ted, what church is it going to be?'

'St Phillip's,' Ted said.

'St Phillip's? I don't know that one. Is that the new one on the corner of Upmeadow?'

'St Phillip's, Chelsea,' Ted said. He squeezed Annie's knee. He was obviously enjoying himself.

'In London?' Mrs Willment said, shocked. 'But I thought you would be getting married from here. I mean, didn't you say Annabel had no family? Surely it doesn't matter to her where she gets married?'

'We want to do it in London so our friends can come,' Ted said.

'Well, what about us?' Mr Willment asked, outraged. 'Think more of your friends than your family, do you?'

'No, Dad, but there'll be more of them than of you, and it's easier for you to travel up to London than for them to travel down here. Besides, it's traditional for the couple to marry from the bride's home, and Chelsea is where Annie lives.'

'Hardly call a flat a home,' Mr Willment grumbled, but Ted had them there. Tradition was right, and should be honoured.

The ordeal was nearly over. After tea, Mr Willment got out his trombone, and he and Ted played a brass duet, called a conversation, while everyone listened and nodded approvingly. Ted was obviously used to this, for he complied with good grace. Then there was a guided tour round the back garden 'while the light holds' with Mrs Willment, and a private conversation about babies, during which that lady elicited the information that Annie wasn't loath to have babies, but on the other hand was quite willing to limit the number by artificial means to suit Ted's income; and then it was half-past nine, and after a last cup of tea they were leaving, getting into Ted's car again, escaping to their own idiosyncratic world beside which the Willments' 'normality' seemed so stifling.

'There,' he said jubilantly as they sped through the dark streets towards the motorway again, 'it's done, and you need never meet them again.'

'Except at the wedding,' she said doubtfully.

'Ah yes, the wedding. I still can't quite believe it's going to happen,' he said. 'I'm afraid to let you out of my sight, in case

119

you turn into fairy mist and dissolve.'

She drew deep breaths to calm herself and restore her sanity, and took his hand and put it back on her leg, where it was comfortable.

'Oh that this too, too solid flesh –? Don't worry, melt I won't. I'm beginning to believe I might be going to marry you. Your family are too real to be imagined.'

'Have you been thinking you're imagining me, then?' he asked.

'All the time. You'll have to prove yourself to me all over again. When we get home.'

'Try and stop me,' he grinned, and pressed his foot down a little harder.


They spent one morning moving the essentials from Annie's flat to the house. The flat was so cheap that they decided she would keep it on, but store her personal gear at Ted's house and use that as the main home. His house was very beautiful and unexpected, a detached, modern house built on the top of Highgate Hill, with a wonderful view over the great park. It had a high walled garden and a private swimming-pool, and was built in the Swedish open-plan style, with the bedrooms – each with a dressing-room and bathroom *en suite* – opening off a balcony that overlooked the huge living area, whose fourth wall was glass from floor to ceiling.

Ted shared the house with its co-owner, an Australian girl who played the cello in one of the London orchestras.

'She won't get in our way,' he told Annie as he showed her his bedroom, which she would now share, of course. The idea was slightly claustrophobic. 'She has her own life. We hardly ever meet as it is – you know what orchestra life is like.'

'What puzzles me is how you could afford a house like this, even with a co-owner. It must have cost a fortune,' Annie said, staring in awe at the huge window-wall, with its view over the rolling parklands of north London.

'She has a very rich lover,' he said. 'I'm a sort of resident caretaker. She'd be afraid to live alone, and he'd be afraid to let her live alone. So here I am. He put up most of the money, but we share the running costs. That's why I can't buy the Ferrari I've always had my heart set on.'

'And this man doesn't mind you being around the house with his mistress?' Annie asked, intrigued. Ted smiled.

'He's met me – he trusts me. I think he thought I was too transparent to be any threat to anyone. And of course, as far as Jenny and I are concerned, he was right. I wouldn't care to mess around there. The set-up is perfectly balanced, and doesn't want disrupting.'

'But I'll be a disruption,' Annie said in a small voice. He put his arms round her.

'Don't start looking for problems again. It will be all right. The house is big enough for three of us not to get on each others' nerves.'

In the course of moving, Annie naturally came across her violin, stored in the bottom of her wardrobe. She drew it out, musician's instinct making her handle it with care, and opened the case. Darkly shining, a thing of beauty, every violin begs to be handled. Hers was rather a special one, having a tiny decoration on the stem in mother-of-pearl – a cluster of pansies. It had a bow to match, similarly decorated.

Annie sat down on the floor, cross-legged, and stroked the fiddle tenderly. It was a kind of lost child to her, the image, the photograph of her old life and of all that might have been. Almost of its own accord, it was raised to her shoulder, and that shoulder instinctively tucked itself round the instrument, and her chin came down comfortably on the rest, wriggling itself into place. It was out of tune, of course, the strings slackened off for its long life in the dark, and she began to tune it, for what musician could endure an out-of-tune instrument?

The sound of the plucked strings seemed very loud in the room after the long silence. She plucked and listened, tightened the pegs, brought the strings up to their playing tautness, tested again, and was satisfied. And there she

121

stopped. There was nothing more she could do. She couldn't play it. With a sigh she was not even aware of, she brought the instrument down from her shoulder and laid it in her lap, and then, glancing up, she saw Ted in the doorway. He had the expression of someone holding his breath for fear of disturbing something very important. She smiled at him briskly and put the fiddle back in its velvet-lined case.

'It's no good looking like that, Ted,' she said. 'You can't turn the clock back.'

'You never know,' he said, maddeningly. 'A change of scene will sometimes work miracles. You might as well keep it, anyway. You'd probably regret it if you sold it.'

She clutched it to her chest in an involuntary movement. 'I'm not selling it,' she said sharply. He smiled encouragingly.

'You see,' he said gently.

'It's not that,' she said awkwardly. 'It's just that – it seems part of me.'

'That's good,' he said. 'That's the way it should be. Shall we take it down to the car? I think we've got everything else now, haven't we?'

'Everything I want to take,' said Annie.

# TEN

From the beginning Annie had been in favour of a quiet wedding with no fuss, but Ted had spoken to her firmly on the subject.

'It's a thing you'll only do once in your life,' he said with what seemed to her to be either naïve optimism or a rather impressive determination. 'So you might as well do it as well as you can, and enjoy it. Besides,' he had added when she had appeared to remain unconvinced, 'you don't want people to think you're not proud of me, do you? Hole-and-corner stuff wouldn't look too good, would it, in certain quarters.'

So it was really not for her own gratification that she was to be married in moderate style, but to please other people – Julie, who had always looked forward to her sister's wedding, at which she hoped to have the fun that she was precluded from having at her own wedding by being the principal girl at it; Ted's family, who evidently expected it; the boys and girls of the orchestra, who deserved a bit of fun in their hard-working lives, and who were all very fond of Ted and wanted the best for him; and finally but not least of all, Ted himself. From the feeling that she was somehow not doing him a favour by marrying him at all, she had a great desire to please him in little ways, and the wedding was a good opportunity.

So there were to be flowers in the church, and hired cars, and a photographer and a lavish wedding-breakfast at Bailey's Hotel. In order to fit in with the orchestra's schedule, it had to be done on a Friday afternoon, rather than the traditional Saturday, but it proved better that way since there was less competition with other weddings, and many of Ted's relations were put off coming at all.

'Which is all to the good,' he told Annie on the Wednesday – their last day at work, 'because most of them are uncouth and boozy old sods, and would very likely wreck the whole thing if they were there in enough strength to lose their inhibitions.'

Annie was busy that day going through things with the assistant concerts manager, a girl called Tracy Dean, who was to do her job while she was away – 'On your honeymoon,' as Tracy insisted on calling it, rolling her eyes romantically. She had not long had her job, and since she was at one remove from the actual bodies, she still looked upon the musicians as rather godlike creatures from another realm, and thought it the height of romanticism for Annie to be actually marrying one of them – particularly Ted, who was handsome and young to boot.

'By the way, have you heard about Ivor?' she said as she and Annie were parting their ways at lunch-time.

'What about Ivor?' Annie asked apprehensively. Since the Angus incident, she had not doubted Ivor's ability to cause trouble when he wished to.

'He's resigned,' Tracy said, watching Annie's face. 'Yes, I thought that would surprise you. The letter arrived this morning just before I left the office.'

'Why is he resigning? What reason did he give?'

'He didn't give a reason. Just said please accept my notice etcetera. But I had it on the grapevine – promise you won't spread it?'

'No. Who told you? Your boss?'

'Phil, yes. Well, Phil said that somebody Very Important had put pressure on the Chairman to get Ivor to resign.'

'Which very important somebody was that?' Annie asked patiently.

'Andrew Barrett,' Tracy said, round-eyed with importance. Andrew Barrett was the conductor thought most likely to get the next appointment as Principal Conductor at the end of the present contract, in the autumn. He had a lot of contacts that would prove valuable to the orchestra and it was almost certain that he would get the appointment. Annie sighed – more political tangles! 'But really,' she said aloud,' I don't see why Ivor should resign. I mean, I can't think what pressure anyone could put on him, unless he has a spare time hobby as a child-molester.'

Tracy giggled. 'Well, he has, and that's all I know. I wonder who we'll get to replace him? Be nice if that Geoffrey Hamilton would stay on. I quite fancy him.'

'God forbid,' Annie said, shuddering. 'Fortunately there's no chance of that. He's wedded indissolubly to the English Sinfonietta. So poor old Ivor's been ivored at last? He who lives by the sword shall die by the sword, or whatever. Poor Angus would be pleased, perhaps.'

On the Thursday night after the concert at the Festival Hall Ted went home to Highgate while Annie travelled on the tube to the Chelsea flat, for it was from those respective places that they were to go to the church the next day. They kissed goodbye lightly in the lift on the way down to the street, and Ted said, 'Don't be late tomorrow, will you?'

'Not even the statutory five minutes?' she teased, and then was sorry, for she could see he was very tightly strung up about the following day's events. She touched his cheek with her finger-tip and said seriously, 'Don't worry. I'll be there with me boots blacked. Don't forget anything essential like the ring or your trousers, will you?'

'After tomorrow, we won't need trousers at all,' he bragged, but his parting smile to her was one of innocence and sweetness. He was not spending his last night of 'freedom' getting drunk. He had played like an angel in the concert, and was now going home to have a hot bath and fall exhausted into bed. Annie knew she could trust him, which was one of his great attractions, and also one of his serious drawbacks.

Julie and Pat arrived at the flat late on Friday morning, and took Annie out to lunch, though she could eat very little, was white and looked as if she might be sick at any moment. The Pat changed his suit quickly and took himself off to inspect the church while the two girls changed their clothes. Annie's dress was an Empire-style frock of cream-coloured muslin and lace, trimmed with coffee ribbon, and with it she had chosen a large, broad-brimmed hat of cream straw trimmed with real flowers. 'It's bad enough marrying in a church at all,' she had said, 'without wearing white and a veil. That would be hypocrisy.'

'A lot of people do,' Julie had replied, 'and compared with them you're an angel.'

'I hardly think that's the point,' Annie had said dryly.

Julie was wearing a plain day-dress and her colours were the reverse of Annie's – coffee dress trimmed with cream – and her hat was smaller and untrimmed, so together they looked stylish and smart and just special enough, without being too dressy. Neither carried flowers. 'I shouldn't know what to do with them,' Annie had protested at the idea. 'I'd feel like a corpse with a lily in its hands.'

'You don't know what a corpse feels like,' Pat had teased her, but she had looked so apprehensive that he had rather wondered.

The girls dawdled over their dressing so as not to have too much time to spare, but still they were ready long before Pat came back, and Pat came back more than early enough to start off for the church.

'I wish I wasn't doing this,' Annie said, staring blankly out of the window.

'Everyone feels like that on their way up the aisle,' Pat assured her.

'Oh, do they?' Julie said menacingly. 'That's the first I've heard of it.'

'You wouldn't have felt it, only because you were still hung over from your hen night,' Pat said. 'Listen, shall we start? It might be better to be driving there slowly than to be sitting here thinking about it. If we're too early we can go around the block.'

'The block,' Annie said, and a grim smile flickered over her face. 'That's what this reminded me of. Anne Boleyn, waiting in her Tower cell for the guards to fetch her to the block. Yes, let's go. It is a far far madder thing I do now, mateys, than I ever thought I'd do, but I can't back out at this stage. For one thing, who'd eat up all that grub?'

\*

126

The church looked splendid, filled with vases of dahlias, purple and scarlet and yellow, and deep crimson roses, and sheafs of gladioli, great open horns of shell-pink and rich cream, and as soon as she came in through the door, Annie was glad that they had ordered flowers after all. They did make a difference. The church, for all that it was so big, seemed almost full, what with Ted's relations and almost all the orchestra being there, as well as various musical and non-musical friends, but Annie's eyes were drawn straight to the two figures standing in front of the altar. Two backs, neatly suited. One, the taller and more slender of the two, was Warren Stacker, asked to be best man by Ted not so much because he was a best friend but because of all the people he knew Warren was the one best able to carry off an occasion with style.

The other, broader and a little shorter, was already unmistakable to her. She saw him begin to turn his head and restrain himself as the organ began the wedding march from Mendelssohn's 'Midsummer Night's Dream'. It was being played by Jimmy Bowyer, the fourth horn in the MSO who played the piano for the orchestra when one was required, and who had studied in Edinburgh on the great cathedral organ. Panic overcame Annie, and she slowed, beginning instinctively to withdraw her hand preparatory to turning and running away as fast as her long dress would let her; but Pat must have known, for his arm, on which her hand was resting, snapped in, holding it tight to his ribs. He was very much stronger than her – she couldn't have got away from him. He glanced down at her, one swift glance which contained warning and reassurance and affection, as he towed her firmly up the aisle to deposit her beside her lover.

As she came to a halt she could actually *feel* Ted trembling across the little space between their bodies, and somehow it gave her courage. A little sideways glance told her that he was as white as she was, though for different reasons, but when their eyes met, he gave her a wonderful, wicked, triumphant grin, and she knew she was hooked. The ceremony continued, and in a little while he was struggling to

127

get the gold ring on her heat-swollen finger, and Annabel Holst (no relation to Gustav) was firmly wedded to Edward George Willment, for better or for worse, and all the rest of it.

Back down the aisle, this time on Ted's hard muscular arm, and four of Ted's trumpet-playing friends, including Bob Akroyd, were playing the most magnificent, soul-thrilling, professional-sounding fanfare, better even than the one played at Princess Anne's wedding.

'Nothing like being in the business,' Ted whispered to her, keeping his lips fixed in a smile for the photographers. 'If one of them had cracked a note he'd never have heard the last of it.'

Annie laughed at this, and at that moment they emerged from the darkness of the church onto the steps, and the photographers were snapping away again. She noticed, gratefully, that the sun had come out and the rain that had threatened, muggily, all day had come to nothing. There was no room on the steps and narrow pavement for taking group pictures, so it was just a case of letting the people with cameras get snaps of Ted and Annie, Ted and Annie with the four trumpeters (repeat performance please), and Ted and Annie with Pat, Julie and Warren, and then Ted shouted, 'All right everybody – the bar's open at Bailey's Hotel.'

A ragged cheer went up, and the foremost members of the orchestra identified themselves by the stampede towards the cars. People began to throw confetti – much to Annie's discomfiture, for she had always despised the habit of chucking fragments of scrap paper over people just because they'd got married – and they ducked through a hail of this to meet worse as they neared the car, for Doris Walker had gone one better and bought rice.

'Ouch!' Ted yipped as he caught a shower about the ears. 'Bloody 'ell, Doris, what do you think we are, pigeons?'

'Think yourself lucky I remembered to take it out of the Pyrex dish!' Doris yelled back, throwing all the harder.

'She's working off her frustrations,' shouted Miss Piggy after them. 'I told her it was supposed to be cooked first, but she said she'd get more reaction this way. Come on, Doris, don't stop to pick it up – we'll be last at the bar.'

'Waste not want not,' they heard Doris reply as they got into the car. 'We've got the whole weekend to go yet.'

'God, what a shower!' Ted laughed happily as they settled themselves in the back seat amid the oppressive smell of confined leather. 'Bless 'em – no chance of a dull party with them around.' He turned to Annie and surveyed her with bright eyes. 'I haven't had time yet to tell you how beautiful you look. Or how much I love you. I was so afraid you wouldn't come, you can't believe how relieved I felt when old Jimmie struck up with the March. And even then – when we went into the vestry and you stopped just as you were about to sign on the dotted line –'

'Oh that,' she said. 'That was only because I wasn't sure what to sign. I've been Annabel Holst so long – do you really want me to change my name to Willment?'

'Only if you want to, dear,' he said, and she interrupted him with a quizzical smile.

'"Dear?" That's the first time you've called me dear. They say that marriage changes people. It seems they're right. We've only left the church five minutes and you're middle-aged already.'

He reached up and picked some rice out of her hat-brim. 'If it were to rain, you'd be bogged down in no time,' he said. 'All right, I won't call you dear. I'll think of something else. But you *are* dear to me. You know that, don't you? Listen, you aren't regretting it, are you? I thought you were going to be sick when you first reached the altar. Pat looked as if he was holding you up.'

'Just nerves,' she said. Gentle lies, what marriage is without them? 'And probably hunger. I couldn't eat any lunch, but now I'm hungry as a horse. I hope we get a chance to eat at this do – from my memory of other people's weddings, the last people to get anything to eat are always the bride and groom.'

'Don't worry, it's a sit-down meal. All very proper and splendid. And the food had better be good, or they'll get

129

some terrible publicity. Did you see the two reporters outside the church?'

'No – how did you know they were reporters?'

'They were writing down names in notebooks, Dumbo. Did you think they had neon signs on their hats?'

'Dumbo now, eh? Well, it's better than dear anyway,' she teased. When the car drew up outside the hotel the driver had to cough loudly to attract their attention. Young love, he thought, is very pretty.

The food *was* good, and Annie got enough to eat and a lot more than enough to drink. There was an elegant speech from Warren, who had probably made it at more weddings than he could remember, and a to-the-point speech from Pat, much cheered for its brevity, and some extremely vulgar, in fact almost unprintable, ones from other members of the orchestra. Mr Willment, who evidently wasn't used to wine, proposed the toast to the happy couple three times, and drank it enthusiastically each time, going on to do a few solo runs when it was clear no one was going to pay any attention to him from then on.

Then the tables were cleared like lightning, and there was dancing to the music of a very talented group made up of members of the orchestra who had arranged a rota between them so that they would all get the chance to circulate, and, what was more important, to get outside of the free booze. Annie, sitting at the table listening to the unrepeatable jokes that were being told, had felt too happily drunk to move, but as soon as the dancing started she found the alcohol flowing about her veins like adrenalin, and she felt she could have danced all night without feeling a thing.

She danced first with Ted as was demanded by tradition.

'Do you realise, this is the first time we've danced together?' she asked. 'What a strange thing.'

'I don't dance very well, I'm afraid.'

'No, you don't.'

'I wasn't taught in school. I can see honesty is going to be the hallmark of this relationship. Anyone else would have said, you dance quite well really, or something like that.'

'I just happen to be a good dancer,' Annie said flippantly. 'Next please. Ah, Warren!'

'Best man's privilege, old son. Sort of *droit de seigneur*,' Warren said, slipping an arm between Annie and Ted and whirling her expertly into his embrace.

'Just keep it clean, mate, that's all,' Ted said, pretending to be angry. 'I want her back in good condition.'

'The very best, old man, no probs,' Warren called imperturbably, and they whirled off round the floor. Warren danced, as he did everything, superbly, and Annie was really enjoying herself, and was sorry to be transferred to the arms of her new father-in-law, who stumped manfully along counting the steps to himself in an audible mutter.

'I hope you'll be very happy together,' he said, sounding doubtful, though he may only have been drunk. 'You should be dancing with him now. I don't like this custom of parting the happy couple so soon.'

'You're parting us yourself,' she pointed out logically. 'Anywrv, there are fifty-six male members of the orchestra here alone, leaving aside all the odds and sods. I don't expect I shall be seeing much of Ted until Saturday afternoon at the earliest.'

This shocked Mr Willment so much that they manoeuvred in grim silence until to their common relief he was excused by Pat.

'Just walk,' Pat said. 'I can't do these fancy steps.'

'I never met an Irishman who *could* dance,' Annie said. They walked in small circles, almost moving on the spot, and Annie leaned gratefully against Pat's familiar comforting bulk. 'Having a nice time?' she asked him.

'Pretty nice. What was that rudeness I heard you saying to poor old man Willment?'

'Rudeness? I was as polite as could be,' she said, puzzled.

'I thought I heard you saying you were going to try out all the male members tonight.'

Annie began to giggle. 'The male members of the orchestra,' she elucidated. 'I hadn't realised it could be taken another way. No wonder the poor old gink was shocked.

131

And then I went on to talk about odds and sods. He must have thought his son married a very odd fish.'

'You're a wicked girl, Annie, and I'm glad a strong-minded working lad has got hold of you. There won't be any liberal nonsense about *that* marriage. I wonder if you fully realise what you've got yourself into?'

Annie glanced up at him, but he was smiling, and she decided he was joking.

'He's all right,' she said. 'Wherever he is. Really, weddings are most extraordinary – the one person you see nothing of is the one you've married.'

After Pat, she had to dance with Bob Akroyd, and then Andy Wayne, David Bastowe, and the other members of London's trumpet-playing fraternity. They were all rather alike to Annie's drink-bemused eyes, pleasant, charming, earthy, broad-shouldered, barrel-chested, lipless, humorous blokes; salt of the earth, she found herself thinking sloppily as she draped herself over yet another broad damp shirt-front. In between dances she sipped thirstily at champagne which, being chilled, made her think it was quenching her thirst. Fortunately she danced vigorously enough to work off the worst of the fumes, so that, though she stayed drunk, she didn't fall down or pass out or throw up, which was just as well.

She was working her way through the string section when a crash of cymbals halted the dancing, and Pat, towering over the crowd sideways as well as upwards, sought her out and fetched her like a runaway child to the top end of the room where Ted, very red in the face and glassy of eye, was standing beside the wedding-cake waiting for her to help him cut it.

'I just found out,' he said to her, rather as if she were a fellow guest instead of one of the principals, of whom he was the other, 'that only the bottom tier is real. The top bits are cardboard under the icing. They do it for all the weddings. Saves money. They've got a spare plain bottom bit in case we run out of cake. Wonderful, what modern science dreams up, isn't it.'

'I rather think you're drunk,' she said carefully.

'I rather think I am, too. Who are you?'

'Not sure,' she said. 'Shall we get on with the cutting?'

They were steered through the bit of ceremony by Pat, who seemed to be able to drink twice as much as everyone else without showing any effects.

'It must be because you're so big,' Annie said. 'More room for the stuff to circulate. Less alcohol per pound.'

'Weight, or sterling?' Ted asked her, and she couldn't decide. Pat pushed them together and launched them onto the floor for the traditional waltz.

'I can do this one,' Ted said happily.

'So you can,' she discovered. They revolved through an erratic first circuit alone on the floor, and then other couples joined them and Annie managed to halt Ted in the corner of the room to say, 'I must go to the loo. It's all that champagne,' and she left him and trotted out into the quietness of the lobby and the seclusion of the cloakroom, which she had to herself. Having relieved herself she washed her hands at the sink and pressed cold water on her face for a long time to cool herself and clear her mind. She was sobering rapidly, for much of it had been the combination of the noise and excitement in the other room. She stared at her reflection in the mirror over the sink. Her level grey eyes looked back impartially, as if they belonged to someone else. You couldn't tell, she thought vaguely, from looking at me.

Tell what?

Anything. I look just the same as always.

But she wasn't the same. She was married now, a married woman, with all that entailed. And suddenly, she didn't want to be. She knew she shouldn't have done it, that her reasons had been inadequate, unfair to Ted, unfair to herself. Panic welled up in her, and she fought it down. She bathed her face again and smoothed her hair with her hands – she had no comb with her. She decided to go up to the room they had booked for the night and change into a dress. She looked down at the cream gown with distaste. Wedding gown! She

133

doubted that even if she dyed it some other colour she would want to wear it again.

Outside again she ran up the stairs, further away from the noise and the music. They were all enjoying themselves. Well, so had she been, at the time. In their room she slipped the dress off, keeping her eyes firmly turned away from the evidences of Ted's presence, his clothes and hairbrush and suitcases and a scatter of small belongings, dropped carelessly and waiting for their master to return. Their master. Her master too, now. She put on a plain, elegant dress of grey crêpe de Chine, and combed her hair loose, and felt better. Her master? She looked at herself in the mirror, her unchanged self, and the idea came to her with stunning clarity and simplicity, that all she had to do was to walk out of the hotel, right then and there, and never come back.

She was still pretty drunk, which accounted for the apparent simplicity of the scheme, for had she been properly cool and sober she would have seen a hundred flaws in it. The idea stuck, and in its grip she put down her brush, picked up the case which was waiting, already packed, for them to set off on their honeymoon the next morning, and her handbag, and walked out of the room and down the stairs.

In the lobby the noise of the party – her wedding-party – reached her ears loud and cheerful, and she paused, sanity beginning to trickle back. And it was while she was standing hesitating thus, that the outside door opened and Geoffrey came in. He looked pretty wild, his hair dishevelled, his shirt open at the neck and sweat-marked under the arms. His trousers were dress trousers – he must have been playing at a concert and come straight from it.

His eyes went straight to her, almost as if he had known she would be standing there. They were leaden, the eyes of a man who has lost everything.

'Well, I see I've come to the right place after all. You *are* getting married here today?'

Annie stared at him as if mesmerised. She jerked her head towards the hulabaloo. 'In there.'

'And what are you doing out here, with a case in your

hand?' he asked, his eyes suddenly coming alive, a smile creeping up one side of his mouth. He laughed suddenly, and it sounded like relief. 'Annie, Annie, don't say you've realised the error of your ways?'

'I was just – I was – I was just going,' she said limply. He took the case from her unprotesting hand, and his voice was unusually soft and caressing as he said, 'Darling Annie, *dushka*, you *were* just going, weren't you? You know, you really can't marry that man. Come on, come with me.'

'What are you doing here?' she found wit to ask.

'I came to fetch you,' he said. 'I came to get you back. Come on, darling, before someone notices you're missing.' And with that he took her hand in his free one, and, forcing himself to walk slowly and calmly, led her out of the hotel into the warm August evening and towards his waiting car.

# ELEVEN

At first she was so shaken and dizzy that all she could do was to lie back in the bucket seat with her eyes closed and get her breath back. She felt like someone who has just had a narrow escape; she was still too fuddled to be aware just how false that feeling was. The car stopped and started, jolted and turned with the vagaries of London streets and traffic and traffic lights, but after a while the movement became smoother and the direction continuous, and Annie was aware in some way that they were travelling very fast.

Cautiously she opened her eyes, and saw that they were driving along a motorway. A moment longer was enough to tell her that it was the M4, and for a mad second she thought perhaps she had dreamed it all, for it was along the M4 that she and Ted would have driven to their honeymoon in the cottage in Wales he had told her about. But the car was not Ted's car; the speed at which they were belting down the fast lane was not Ted's speed; and slowly, almost reluctantly, she turned her head to regard her driver, who was emphatically not Ted.

He drove well – it had always given her a strange kind of thrill to be driven by him. He kept very still, sitting right back in the seat so that his arms and legs were at full stretch and his whole body was braced to the weight of the car. His hands on the steering-wheel were strong and capable, his eyes looked steadily ahead, alert, aware, flicking without fuss from time to time to the rear-view mirror. He drove with concentration. It reminded her of the way he played; it was almost dedicated.

His concentration gave her the opportunity to study him again or, rather, to feast her eyes on him again. That profile she knew so well, from being driven by him on a hundred, a thousand journeys: the slight crest of dark hair, sprinkled with grey now, overhung a high, broad forehead, a forehead that was growing progressively higher as his hair receded from it; the neat, straight Grecian nose and firm, rounded chin gave distinction to his outline, which would otherwise have been marred by the slightly crooked, lipless mouth – a brass-player's mouth, but to the lay observer merely ugly; and beneath unexpectedly bushy eyebrows, young eyes of Siamese-cat blue gazed levelly and slightly cynically at the world.

He was, except for his mouth, a handsome man. He was wealthy, and dressed well, his figure elegant and showing off good clothes to advantage; his manners were smooth and social; he was knowledgeable and witty and charming. From the very beginning, Annie had been slightly at a loss as to why such a man, a man who could choose from the whole world, should choose her. But it was a long time since she had seen him with the eyes of an impartial observer. Though she knew in a vague way that he was generally considered handsome and charming, to her he was a giant figure in her mind, a way of life, a condition of her thoughts. He was just Geoffrey to her, and the word needed no further explanation to her brain.

His eyes did not move from their forward direction, but he must have known she had opened her eyes, for he said quietly, 'Are you all right now?'

'Yes,' she said. 'I just feel a little flattened.'

'You should feel, on the contrary, inflated. But I think I understand.'

'Where are we going?' The question seemed to surprise him a little.

'Where? To Henley, of course,' he said, raising an eyebrow. Henley was where he had his out-of-town house, a beautiful Georgian brick building, with stables, and terraced gardens down to the river, an orchard, and several acres of paddocks. It was there that Shona and Sacha had their 'home' when they were in England.

'But isn't – I mean, what about Shona?' Annie asked nervously. He smiled then, the corner of his mouth nearest to her lifting wryly.

138

'My dearest child, you don't think I'd be taking you there if Shona was in residence? Of course she's not there! She's gone to Scotland for three weeks, or perhaps longer. You know that her sister is looking after her now?'

Shona had always had need of a nurse-companion, since Geoffrey was so little at home.

'I didn't know,' Annie said.

'Yes, Morag got divorced recently, and was proud of it too – you know what these strong-minded Scottish women are like. We'd just lost our last hired nurse – to get married, ironically enough – and Morag suggested she came and lived with us, with her brat, and took care of Shona for her keep. It seemed a very suitable arrangement. Shona is happier with a member of her family, and you can expect more from a relative than you could from someone you are paying. So now Morag's taken her up to Scotland for a holiday – to Perth, where they grew up. A nostalgia trip.'

'But doesn't she need a trained nurse around her any more?' Annie asked.

'Morag was a nurse before she married, and the amount she knows is sufficient. It isn't as if Shona was really in need of constant nursing now.'

'I see.' Annie paused, wondering how to frame the next question. 'And what about – I mean, is –'

Now he did flick her a glance, and there was a wealth of kindness in it, the sort of kindness she was not accustomed to receive from him.

'No. He's with them. It's the school holidays, of course. He gets on quite well with Morag's Andrew, and he was quite keen to see his mother's birthplace –' It was said before he could stop himself, but he realised at once how stupid he had been, and could have kicked himself. She turned her head away defensively. 'Sorry,' he said abruptly. 'Heat of the moment. I don't usually put my foot in my mouth.'

'It doesn't matter,' she said, and relapsed into silence.

'What matters is,' he said several miles further along, as if there had been no pause, 'that we're together again. My God, when I heard – you couldn't think how I felt. And

139

trapped as I was, I couldn't escape to do anything about it.'

'How *did* you hear?' she asked.

He smiled grimly. 'Ivor told me.'

'Ivor Hotchkiss?' She was amazed. 'How? When? Where?'

'At the concert, my dear, during the interval. He'd come to see the conductor, Andrew Barrett. Hoping for advancement. Barrett wouldn't see him, so in the interval he came along to pump me. He had a kind of feeling that I had some influence with Barrett and might be willing to use it on his behalf.'

'And was he right?'

'Right in the first part and wrong in the second. What he didn't know at first, though he began to guess at it in the end, was that it was I who persuaded Barrett to get him chucked out.'

'Did you? *Did* you? I'm amazed. What influence have you got with Barrett then?'

'He and I are on the boards of several of the same companies. I put a lot of money his way. I could also make things quite awkward for him in many ways. I'm a friend it pays him to keep.'

Annie digested this. The slimy side of life, perhaps. So different from the world in which she and most of the rest of the population lived. Riches bring with them, it seemed, complications of that kind.

'But why did you do it? Why did you get Ivor the push?'

Geoffrey smiled. 'I fancied a change. I wanted the job myself.'

'Because I was there?' she asked in a small voice.

'Not entirely, though I admit that did have its attractions for me. Are you disappointed? Perhaps you would have liked me to risk all for love?'

'I wouldn't want you to have done things like that for love,' she said. 'And I don't believe you are capable of that kind of love anyway. Above all, you're a practical man.'

'You're right, of course. Well, Ivor didn't wonder about my reasons. He's far too emotional, that man – he'll never

140

make the top. And, happy to be able to pay me back in what he thought was kind, he told me that at that very moment you were getting married to that pathetic Ted Wilmot—'

'Willment,' Annie corrected firmly. Geoffrey did not acknowledge the correction.

'– and having a reception at Bailey's before rushing off on honeymoon. I think he was rather frightened by the reaction he got – it was more than he bargained for. There I was, trapped by the second half! I was playing, I couldn't get off, and I was terrified that you'd have gone away before I could get there. As soon as the concert was over I was off the platform like a bullet from a gun, into my car, and driving like a maniac to Gloucester Road. If a police-car had spotted me –! And when I went in through the swing doors, there you were, standing at the bottom of the stairs with your case in your hand, just as if you'd been waiting for me to arrive and fetch you away.' He laughed jubilantly at the thought. 'It must have been arranged – Fate, or something. Maybe you heard me calling you. Do you remember how you used to know what I was thinking – and vice versa? We'd both come out with the same sentence at the same moment?'

Annie nodded, too moved to speak at once.

'And the times I'd phone you up just as you were lifting the phone to call me?' he went on.

'And that time I was terribly ill and you got a strong premonition that I was in trouble,' Annie remembered. He nodded, reaching one hand out to her, which she caught and squeezed.

'I remember that,' he said. 'It was a bad moment for me. It just came over me like blind panic. I had to find out what had happened to you.' There was silence for a while, as they both thought of the strange closeness there had been between them over the years. Then he said, 'I was always content to know you were just somewhere in the world with me, breathing the same air and looking at the same sky. If you had died, I don't know what I would have done. In some strange way I don't understand, you are important to me – do you understand me? When I heard you were going to get

141

married, I couldn't stand it. You belong to me, I can't let anyone else have you. So I had to come and get you back.'

'Like a lost wallet,' Annie said. He smiled, squeezing her hand again before withdrawing it to the steering-wheel.

'If you like. A wallet with all my credit cards in it, anyway.'

'Credit cards are easily replaced,' she said.

'And some photographs of great sentimental value, that *can't* be replaced,' he added, and she laughed.

The house was empty and silent, but there was no air of desertion. It felt comfortable and lived in. He took her into the library, where one lamp had been left alight to welcome him home, throwing a soft and muted glow over the fine old furniture and the leather-and-gilt spines of innumerable books. On a table there was a decanter of whisky, a Thermos of hot black coffee, and a plate of *foie gras* sandwiches.

'All left for me by the daily woman,' Geoffrey said. 'I hate to come back to an empty house with nothing to welcome me. Sit down, be comfortable. I'll fetch another cup.'

Ten minutes later, refreshed and comforted by the food and drink, they went up the stairs to bed. Geoffrey didn't put the light on, for there was enough starlight to undress by. Annie took her clothes off and slid in between the clean cool sheets, and in the dark Geoffrey went to open the window, letting in the fresh night smells of grass and dew, before quickly undressing and climbing into bed beside her.

He leaned across her, and the familiar smell of his skin made her heart lurch crazily.

'Annie,' he whispered, and to her amazement she could feel that he was trembling. 'Annie, my darling, my own darling.' His shape blocked out the light, and then his warm, hard lips were brushing hers and his hands were stroking the slender column of her neck, her smooth shoulders, her full round breasts. She lifted her arms around his neck and drew him down to her, aching with longing, and with a quivering sigh he slipped into her, coming home after a long exile. Her lips opened under his and their tongues met like old friends as he began to move.

'Annie, I love you,' he cried softly, as if despite himself, as they reached the climax together; and later, as they were drifting out into sleep, tumbled gratefully together, limbs entwined, he murmured, 'Never leave me.'

Annie smiled, and slept.


Annie was woken the next morning at some unearthly hour by the unfamiliar racket of the dawn chorus. Her mind panicked, she lay rigid on her back, staring at an utterly unknown ceiling without the least idea of where she was or how she got there.

'God,' she said, while her brain flapped like a dying fish. There was an answering grunt from beside her, she turned her head and saw Geoffrey – *Geoffrey?* – and then memory flooded back. The relief was only momentary. Almost as soon as she realised where she was, she realised what a terrible thing she had done.

Slowly she went back over the events of the previous day, wondering at what point the thing had become possible. I was very drunk, she thought, but there was no comfort in that either. Even drunk she should not have been capable of such enormity – and in any case, she had not been *that* drunk, not so drunk that she was not aware of what she was doing.

Only so drunk that she didn't care. It had been her wedding night, last night – she had spent her wedding-night with her lover. She was married to – Ted. His image burst into her brain like a lightning flash, his face, his gentle eyes reproaching her. She had left him without a word, abandoned him on their wedding-day to run off with another man. Without even telling him where she was going.

What would he be thinking? What would he be suffering? She groaned. She had never wanted to hurt him, but the hurt he would be suffering now must be dreadful! He might at first think she had been kidnapped, or had fallen down somewhere and hurt herself and was waiting to be rescued; or had gone off in a brainstorm and drowned herself in the Thames;

or had got herself run over, or had suffered from amnesia and was wandering friendless in some shabby suburb.

All those things would probably have run through his frantic mind before he either guessed or found out the truth. Ivor would make sure that sooner or later he found out who had taken her away, and how willingly. The hotel staff, of course, might have seen her leave, might be able to furnish enough of a description to leave him in little doubt as to what had happened.

And then what would he think. Oh God, oh God, poor Ted, she thought, covering her face with her hands. What had she done? How could she have hurt him like that, her kind, loving Ted who had never wanted anything but to make her happy. Her husband, even. She groaned again, and rolled over on to her side – and came up against Geoffrey.

Then the other half of her mind took over, and was singing with joy. He loved her. What a proof of love he had given her last night! On hearing that she really was getting married to Ted, he had been driven so wild with love for her that he had driven like a bat out of hell to snatch her away and bring her to his own home so that he might keep her and no one else might have her. He loved her, by that proof, more even than she loved him, for she had been willing to marry Ted, would have gone through with it if he had not come and taken her away.

And here he was beside her, close to her, loving her. She loved him so irrationally much that simply to be near him was a great joy. The birdsong was fading, and she was still very, very tired. She nudged up against him, passing an arm across him. He grunted and snuggled in his sleep, and caught the hand that she put round him and pulled it to his breast, and, still smiling, she went back to sleep, curled spoon-wise into his back.

She woke again later – by the strength of the sun she guessed it must be at least nine o'clock – and found him looking at her.

144

'Hello,' he said. 'So you are still here. I thought at first I must have dreamt it.'

'I've been through that bit too,' she said. 'When I first woke I hadn't a clue where I was. There's nothing so doomlike as waking in a strange bed at dawn with a hangover.'

'Have you got a hangover?'

'No, not now. It was only waking up too soon.'

'Good. Because I'm starving – I want a huge breakfast. Come here, though, first, and kiss me.' A long silence. 'That's better. I wanted that even more than food. Oh, sorry, is my beard too rough for you? Your poor chin's going pink. Shall I shave first?'

'First? Before what?' she asked stupidly. He smiled and reached out to stroke her breasts. 'Oh,' she said.

'On second thoughts, I don't think I can wait to shave,' he said, and turned over towards her.

A noise downstairs woke them from the light doze they fell into afterwards, and Annie stiffened in panic. Geoffrey woke and stroked her hair soothingly.

'It's all right, it's only Mrs Harris. The one who left the sandwiches yesterday. You're quite safe. I'm going to shower and shave. Do you want to bath while I shower? It's more companionable.'

It must be something, she thought as she followed him into the bathroom, that he couldn't share with his wife. The water was marvellously hot, and there were loads of wonderful towels, as big as sheets and as thick as carpets. Geoffrey, shaved and shining clean, came and rubbed scented oil into her back and legs for her.

'You must oil your skin when you've been sunbathing,' he reproved her. 'There's nothing tires out skin more than sun.'

He looked so different now he was spruced up. Unshaven, tousled and gummy-eyed, he had looked every bit of the extra age he had over Ted. One has to love someone very much, Annie reflected, to love them looking like that first thing in the morning. Back in the bedroom he dressed rapidly and ran downstairs, telling her to join him when she was ready.

'I'm going to see about that breakfast,' he said. Annie, left alone, began to be nervous, and she lingered over the choosing and putting on of her clothes to delay the moment when she would have to go downstairs and face whatever there was to be faced. When she was finally ready, she crept down the stairs with great caution, listening for any sounds, but the house was quiet, the sun sliding in through the windows and bringing the sound of birdsong from the fragrant gardens.

She opened one door with infinite caution, and found an empty sitting-room. Another door was the kitchen, also empty – she straightened a little with relief, thinking the daily woman must have gone. The third door she tried was the right one, revealing a dining-room with a long polished table and french windows open on to a lawn at the far end. Geoffrey was sitting at the table drinking orange juice and reading a paper. He looked up at her and smiled.

'Come in, sit down, you're just in time.'

She entered and shut the door behind her, and then froze, the closing of the door revealing a woman standing at the sideboard looking round expectantly at her.

'This is Mrs Harris,' Geoffrey said. 'Sit down here beside me. Would you like cereal? Mrs Harris, some cornflakes for Mrs Wilmot.'

Annie sat, and glared at him, knowing this mood of old. Nothing was sacred when Geoffrey was being devilish. Mrs Harris placed a bowl of cornflakes in front of her and asked her if she wanted tea or coffee. She was quite different from the conventional image that 'daily women' conjured up, being a smart-looking woman in her early forties, with an attractive face and figure and iron-grey hair in a kind of modified Eton crop that made her look rather dashing. Annie asked for coffee and ate her cornflakes with a subdued air. Geoffrey continued to read.

Having removed the cereal bowls Mrs Harris served them both with a cooked breakfast and quietly left the room. At once Geoffrey threw down his paper, reached over and lifted her hand to his mouth and kissed it.

'Don't worry,' he said. 'Mrs Harris is paid to mind her own business. She neither says nor even thinks anything of it. You are my guest, that's all. Now eat your nice breakfast. Mrs Harris cooks scrambled eggs the way they should be cooked.'

The words brought Angus briefly and painfully to Annie's mind. The scrambled eggs were delicious, and with them went bacon, small pork chipolatas, mushrooms and tomatoes. Annie discovered she was famished, and cleared the plate in no time. Her wedding-breakfast was a long way behind her, and the *foie gras* sandwiches were the merest dream. Geoffrey plied the coffee-pot, and they finished off with toast and honey and fresh fruit while Geoffrey read bits out of the paper to her as if he knew her mind needed occupying.

'Now then,' he said at last when they were lingering over the last drops of excellent coffee, 'what shall we do today? By one of those occasional perfect arrangements with Fate, I have the day free. Would you like to take a picnic on the river? I've a very comfortable small boat in the boathouse.' He looked at her quizzically. 'Or would you prefer to ride? Whatever you prefer. I want this to be a happy day for you. After all, it is your honeymoon.'

'Oh Geoffrey!' Annabel shook her head at him, torn between amusement and exasperation. 'I suppose you didn't know that we were going to ride in the Welsh mountains for our honeymoon?'

'No, I didn't. I must say that shows rather more imagination and taste than I would have expected from your *husband*.' Annie winced at the casual use of the word, but it only made Geoffrey smile more wickedly. 'It's strange having you as a married woman. Tell me, is adultery more exciting than fornication? Now we can be doubly naughty, and get double the thrill out of daring social conventions.'

'Geoffrey, please stop,' she said. 'I'll have to speak to him

147

– phone him at least. He'll be frantic with worry. If only to let him know I'm all right, I must speak to him.'

'Dear heart, he'll know you're all right,' Geoffrey said seriously. 'He'll know that you went willingly. Don't forget the desk clerk must have seen you leave.'

'He might not have been looking. Besides, haven't you ever seen films where the kidnapper puts a gun in the person's back and tells them to act normally?' Geoffrey was grinning openly now at her reference to films. 'All right, it may seem silly to you, but put yourself in his shoes. For all we know, he might have gone to the police.'

'My dearest girl, you are free to do anything you want, up to and including leaving this very minute. If you want to phone him, phone him. I just don't want you to be upset, that's all. Won't tonight do? I've a notion that if you get talking to him, it might blight your day. Or perhaps you'd like me to do the phoning?'

'Perish the thought,' she said hastily. 'I can imagine what you'd say to him.'

'Yes, perhaps that would rather be adding insult to injury. Well, what about an anonymous message? Mrs Harris would oblige. That should satisfy you that he isn't worrying unnecessarily about you, without putting you to the ordeal of speaking to him yourself.'

'Perhaps that would be best, though it sounds rather cowardly,' Annie said.

'Not cowardly – merely a sensible precaution. You shouldn't talk to him until you're in an emotionally calm frame of mind.'

She agreed rather reluctantly. 'What should I tell him?' she asked.

'Whatever you like. What do you mean?' Geoffrey was puzzled.

'I mean, do I tell him that I've run off for a few days holiday? Or that I've found my ideal mate? What are *your* plans? Your plans for our future, I mean.'

Geoffrey hesitated for a moment, and her heart sank. Then he took her hand and stroked it, and said, 'I don't want

148

to talk about that now, either. For much the same reasons. All I want is for us to enjoy a little peace and quiet together. We'll talk about the future later. But you can tell him, if you like, that it won't be my fault if you and I are ever separated again.'

It was the reassurance she wanted, that she hadn't given up everything for a mere one night of pleasure. Yet it left her curiously unreassured. She had reached the stage of her life where she had to make her own decisions, and reassurance could only come from herself, and from the knowledge that she was doing the right thing. Happy as she was to be with Geoffrey, she couldn't yet be sure of that.

# TWELVE

Annie was never again as happy as she was that first day, and she came to look back on it, for all its imperfections, with longing. A message, concocted between them, was sent off via Geoffrey via Mrs Harris to Ted, and though no reply came back by that or any other source, word filtered through the famous grapevine that he had been horribly, horribly upset but had, with grim self-control, cut short his granted leave – since there was no longer any point in taking it – and had gone back to work. Annie had an idea of the courage it would take to face the rest of his work-mates, whether sympathetic or mocking.

She had to face a great many curious stares herself, for Geoffrey had to work on the Sunday, and since he did not want to let her out of his sight, and she could not bear to be alone, she accompanied him. It was some time since she had last seen the English Sinfonietta, but a great many of the personnel were the same, and there were enough people there who remembered when she used to trot along at Geoffrey's heels years ago, and enough who knew something of their history together, to make it extremely embarrassing to meet them again. In particular Bob Akroyd gave her some very old-fashioned looks, and spoke to her, when he was obliged to speak at all, with cold disapproval.

Annie knew that news of her would go back to Ted via that source if no other, but Ted never made any attempt to get in touch with her, either by letter or message or telephone. It seemed he had abandoned her to her own devices, whether having given her up for lost or hoping she would see sense in her own time she didn't know. Life with Geoffrey was not all bliss. Being with him eased an ache she had lived with for so long she had almost forgotten it was there; but though he evidently liked to have her around him, he soon grew used enough to her presence to stop expressing it openly. And nothing this side of the grave would change him or his ways. He led his own life, often leaving Annie somewhwhere like a burdensome child while he went off on his own business, collecting her again afterwards with no query as to how she had spent her time or news as to how he had spent his. Many of his friends were people unknown to her, and she had all the heartache of seeing him surrounded by beautiful, elegant women who hung on his every word with a gross flattery to which he responded with sallies of wit, enjoying it all with great gusto.

At the end of two weeks they moved into his London flat, and Annie was able without too much trouble to deduce that this was because Shona was coming home. She discovered she was right when, one Sunday afternoon when they had just arrived back from a rehearsal for the concert that evening, Geoffrey told her he was going out.

'Must you?' she asked, not anxious to spend a Sunday afternoon alone. She had no friends – she dared not even contact Julie and Pat, for fear of their disapproval – and nowhere to go.

'I must,' he said. 'I have to see Shona. I'll go straight from there to the concert. I'll see you tonight.'

'I'll meet you at the hall, then?' she said. He looked unconcerned, though his words were, 'No, don't do that. You had better not come to the hall, because I promised to take Sacha tonight. It would be better if you and he didn't meet, in case you find yourself unable to resist temptation. I'll take him home after the concert and then come back here, so I'll be quite late.'

It was a miserable, empty afternoon, imagining them all together, Geoffrey and his wife and child. When the time grew near for the concert, she found herself terribly restless, unable to settle to read or watch television. She kept glancing at the clock and imagining how far on their journey they had gone. She had a terrible desire to go along there and, from some place of concealment in the crowd, take a look at the child. She longed to see how he had grown up; surely there could be no harm in just seeing him? She even got as far as

152

dressing and making up her face – but she knew she couldn't do it, that she mustn't do it. She knew that she would not be able to resist going farther than just looking at him, with disastrous consequences, both to the child and herself.

In the end she went to bed with a book, but never got beyond the first page, lying staring at the ceiling and thinking about the mess she was in, and wondering what would become of her. Geoffrey arrived back very late and very tired, and said nothing about Shona or Sacha, his visit or the concert. He merely said he was very tired, asked her if she had set the alarm, and got into bed to sleep. She wanted very badly to know if he had spoken to Shona about the future, but she didn't know how to ask him. More than anything she dreaded his indifference. Suppose he hadn't, that would be worst of all.

She was aware that in typical Geoffrey fashion he had moved with her to London in order to avoid bringing matters to a head when Shona came back from Scotland. If he and Annie had been there when Shona got home, everything would have had to be brought out into the open and discussed. The trouble was, Shona knew that Geoffrey would always have other women, since it was hardly fair that she should expect him to remain without sex for the rest of his life. And therefore, unless Geoffrey said anything to the contrary, she was likely to think that Annie was just another addition to his address book.

Sometimes in the week that followed Annie considered forcing the issue and asking Geoffrey what they were going to do; at other times she thought she ought to leave him and start all over again, this time following Julie's unheeded advice and giving the musical world a wide berth. She had certainly lost her job – she could never go back to the Met Symf again, after this – and all her friends were members of one orchestra or another. It would mean a completely clean start. And yet, what was the point? That way she would lose Geoffrey as well, leaving herself with nothing. No, when it came down to it, Geoffrey was all she had now, and there was no point in doing anything but simply being with him.

153

She could not even get a job, since that would mean being parted from Geoffrey for most of the time, his hours not coinciding with ordinary business hours. So she went with him to rehearsals and recording sessions and concerts, sat by while he practised, ate with him, slept with him, and sometimes waited in cafés or at the flat when he went off on his mysterious business visits when she was not welcome. It was a life of alternate bliss and misery.

At the end of September the English Sinfonietta was going to California to take part in a festival of music, and, since some of the orchestra spouses were going along, it was not difficult for Geoffrey to arrange to take Annie.

'We must get you lots of new clothes, my darling. The things you have are all right in their way, but they're not the things to be seen in in Los Angeles. I want to show you off when we get there. L.A. society is amongst the richest and most brilliant anywhere in the world. I've got a lot of contacts there. You shall go to parties and dinners and receptions the like of which you have never even dreamed of.'

Annie smiled at the idea. 'How will you fit in any concerts with that social programme.'

'With difficulty,' he said airily, 'But I'll do my best. Can't let the ES down, can I?' He caught her round the waist and swung her into a crazy waltz round the sitting-room. 'I can't wait to get you over there! I'm beginning to hate London – so claustrophobic. Everyone . knows everyone else. Dull women, boring men, dreadful covering-up clothes! I long for some sunshine. And I shall be so proud of you. They'll think you a great beauty, you know – the women are very well groomed over there, but they admire English beauty enormously. They don't have any features, just suntans and hairstyles. Not a nose or mouth among them. I shall have my work cut out keeping you to myself!'

His enthusiasm was rather catching, and she found herself thinking of clothes and parties as if they were important. But there was an excuse for it – without it being absolutely said, she knew that he was looking forward to the openness with which he would be able to introduce her into a new society, rather than the half-secretive way they had to go about things here. It encouraged her to open the subject she had more or less instinctively avoided up till then.

'Geoffrey,' she said, 'what are we going to do?'

He stopped in mid-flow of spirits and looked at her, his expression gradually straightening as he realised she was seriously expecting an answer this time. He sighed, and said, 'I've been afraid you were going to ask that.'

'Why afraid?' she said. 'You said yourself – that first day – that we'd talk about the future later. We never have. You must have known we would have to talk sooner or later.'

'I've thought about it, of course – what do you take me for? However it may seem to you, I don't do things lightly, not at this stage of my life, with so much to lose. My responsibilities are enormous, and whatever the magazines might say, life isn't really permissive in society. I've thought about it a great deal. I simply hoped you would think about it too, and come to your own conclusions.'

'The same conclusions as you, you mean? Well, evidently I haven't, if you think nothing needs explaining. So perhaps you'd better tell me what your conclusions are.'

He looked at her consideringly, and then took her hand and sat down with her on the sofa. If this was meant to reassure, it had the exact opposite effect, for she couldn't help feeling that something very bad was to come if he thought she needed to sit down to hear it. She misunderstood him. He merely wished to be assured of her attention, but she didn't know it.

'My darling, things have been difficult for you. They have for me too, though perhaps not as difficult. One way and another, we've been kept apart by various circumstances. Well, I've done my best for us now – we're together, and together most of the time. We can stay together, if we want. Nothing holds us but wanting to be with each other.'

'What you're trying to say, in a roundabout way,' Annie

suggested, 'is that we must just go on the way we are. Is that right?'

'Yes, I suppose so.'

'Why suppose? You must know what you mean?'

'I know what I mean, but I don't entirely know what you mean. What did you want, besides being with me, which I suppose you *do* want, or you wouldn't be here?'

'I thought you would speak to Shona about us. I thought you intended to regularise the situation.'

'*Regularise?* What a lovely expression. I suppose you mean you want us to get married?'

'Eventually, I suppose, yes, that's what I mean. You say I belong to you. Then why not make it public? I don't want to be hidden like a shameful secret all our lives.'

He pressed her hand and said quickly, 'Not that, darling, never that. But just think about it for a minute. Think about my responsibilities. You know that if Shona hadn't been – if the accident hadn't happened, I would have divorced her and married you. I told you that at the time.'

'Yes, you did,' she said – she didn't add that she had never been sure how serious he was when he said it.

'But the accident did happen. Whatever the courts said, it was my responsibility, if it wasn't my fault, that Shona was crippled. A young girl, younger than you. How could I divorce her? You know I couldn't.'

'I know that. I know you couldn't *then* – but things are different now. What use has she got for you now? You hardly ever see her. You don't sleep together. She has her own life, with her companion – her sister now – and you don't enter into it. If you divorced her, she'd still see as much of you. It couldn't make any difference to her. You surely don't imagine I'd object to you going to see her? I'd even go and see her myself.'

He watched her quizzically through this speech. 'And what about Sacha? You seem to have left him out of your calculations. What would happen to Sacha when I divorced his mother?'

'*I am his mother!*' The words came out as a kind of muted

scream, shocking them both into a moment's silence. She bit her lip to stop it trembling and said again in a quieter voice. 'I am his mother. You have forgotten that.'

'He doesn't know that. To all intents and purposes, Shona is his mother. Think of the traumatic effect on him if his father were to abandon his mother, she being a cripple, to marry someone else. I couldn't do it to him, Annie. I love that boy, whatever you may think.'

Annie felt tears running down her face, and she wiped them away with an angry gesture. She didn't want to cry, knowing it would fog the issue.

'You don't think he would accept me as your new wife without being told who I was?'

He looked at her long and hard. 'You couldn't keep it up. You'd have to tell him in the end. And if you didn't, I would. And that would make it all the worse. No, I can't publicly abandon her. I'm not a moral man, but I have a kind of code of my own. I couldn't do it, Annie. I'm sorry.'

She knew there was no more arguing to be done on that point. Quietly she said, 'What had you intended, then?'

'Just to go on as we are. Gradually to work you into the pattern of our lives. As the boy gets older, he'll come to understand that the relationship between you and me is a possible one and doesn't affect my relationship with his mother.' Neither of them had any longer the need to correct this statement. 'She will be my wife. You will be my tacitly acknowledged mistress. We'll live here, and they'll live in the country. I'll spend my time between the two homes. I'll try to make sure neither of you suffers. It's a compromise. All of life's a compromise. You should know that, Annie. You've had enough of the rough end of the stick.'

She gazed past him with sad eyes. 'Your mistress,' she said. 'Well, that's what I am, I suppose. And what about children?'

'Children?' he hadn't seemed to expect that question. 'What children?'

'Any children you and I might have. What would their status be?'

157

He did not meet her eyes now. 'No children, Annie. I don't want any more children. It would complicate things far too much.'

'I see,' she said. She stood up and walked away, to the window and then to the fireplace, aimlessly touching things with her finger-tips. He watched her, his heart aching. At last he stood up and went to her, turning her round and pulling her almost roughly into his arms.

'Annie, darling, my darling, don't be so sad. We've got all our lives together, think of that! We can be together all the time, and that's what's important, isn't it? What do names matter? What's between us nothing can touch. Nothing, do you understand?'

She pressed herself against him for a moment, and then drew back, forcing herself to smile.

'Yes, I understand,' she said. 'I'd better start looking over my clothes for California, hadn't I? And tomorrow we'll go shopping, shall we? That'll be fun.'

'Of course it will. That's right, my good girl. Come on, let's go out somewhere cheerful for a bite of supper. Everything's going to be all right. We'll have fun, you'll see.'

On the eve of flying out to California, Annie couldn't sleep. Geoffrey, beside her, slept busily the sleep of the righteous, but her mind wandered again and again over that long conversation and the implications of it. She had won, Annie thought, that woman whom she couldn't hate. Fighting unfairly with weapons it was impossible to match. She felt absurdly lonely, considering her chosen man was in bed beside her. She thought suddenly of Ted, and wondered how he was feeling, whether he had got over her by now. Perhaps he was in bed with someone else at this very minute – after all, he was an attractive man. And what, oh what, had he said to his family about her? It must have been dreadful for him.

On a crazy impulse she got up, careful not to wake Geoffrey, and went out into the hall where the telephone was. The light from the glass panel of the front door shone on it, spotlighting it almost, as if to show her what she should do. She walked towards it, her eyes apprehensively fixed on it as if it were a dangerous animal. Her hand crept out, hesitated, and lifted the receiver. The *ping* of the bell and the heavy burring of the dialling tone sounded horribly loud in the quietness, and she thought Geoffrey must hear, but he didn't stir.

Carefully, quietly, she dialled the number, running the dial back with her finger after each digit to hush the noise. There was a long pause and a click and then the ringing tone, but it rang only once before the phone was picked up at the other end. It was as if he had been waiting for the call.

'Hello?' His voice, familiar to her. Until she heard it, she had not thought about what she would say. Now she heard it, she knew there was nothing she could say. Yet she could not put the phone down. It was contact, she was lonely. She wanted to talk to him, or to be talked to by him.

'Hello?' he said again. 'Who is it?' She still said nothing, and in a panic began to put the phone down. As if he had seen her, he said suddenly, urgently, 'Annie, is it you? Annie, answer me! Don't put the phone down. Please, Annie.'

Tears flowed from her eyes. She replaced the receiver, not caring now about the noise of its bell, and went back to the bedroom. Geoffrey had not stirred. She got into bed beside him and, contrary to all expectations, fell at once into a deep, dreamless sleep.


Los Angeles was marvellous. The people there seemed to live twice as fast as ordinary mortals, and spend twice as much money as even the richest person anywhere else. The pace of life was hectic for Annie and Geoffrey particularly, for Geoffrey had all the sessions of the orchestra to attend, and in addition took Annie to beach parties and sightseeing during the daytime breaks, and to glittering, celebrity-packed parties in the evenings after concerts. They found little time to sleep, but it didn't seem to matter too much. The wonderful sunshine seemed to invigorate them.

The concerts were astonishing. They were held in the

159

Hollywood Bowl, the great outdoor auditorium fringed with trees that kept out most of the extraneous noise of that noisiest of cities. It was like a fairy-tale scene, with the orchestra playing on the brightly lit platform behind the fountains and fish-pools, and the audience sitting in their little booths, with chairs and tables, under the stars, eating their picnic suppers and drinking champagne or chilled white wine as they listened to the music. It seemed a wonderful idea to Annie, especially as in Los Angeles the weather could be relied upon to an extent that made an English person feel underpriviledged.

The weather accounted for other things too – the size and design of the beautiful houses to which they went after the concerts, for one thing. It would have been ludicrous to build rooms as large as that in houses you would need to heat through a cold winter. Parties were often held outside, in what the Americans confusingly called the backyard, meaning the back garden, or on a terrace lit with fairy lights, or beside the pool. Often they were invited to barbecues, where the amount of meat they were expected to get through would have cost a fortune in England, and the drinks were extraordinary and exotic cocktails with strange names.

Thanks to Geoffrey they were moving in the top rank of society, and the parties were held in houses in the Beverly Hills or Santa Monica districts. Annie's new dresses, chosen by Geoffrey, of course, were not a bit too rich for the occasions, and she found, as he prophesied, that she was much admired, though this too often meant being pressed to some portly middle-aged stomach for the duration of a dance for her liking. She met several film actors and directors, and three well-known novelists, as well as the musical celebrities of the city. What particularly pleased her, however, was that here she was taken for granted, not hidden away, and it was 'Geoffrey and Annabel' as naturally as if they were an old married couple.

Geoffrey did not neglect to show her the sights either. They visited Disneyland and the Grand Canyon, the

160

Observatory and the Paramount film studios, drove up the Santa Clara Valley, and viewed the lights of Los Angeles from the highest point in Beverly Hills. Annie loved bathing from the golden beaches under the blue skies – she had never seen such blue skies; and she had never seen so many shooting stars in her life before as she saw in the course of one warm evening there.

At the end of the second week she was very brown and very thin – despite the huge and lavish meals, for the heat killed her appetite and she was on the go the whole time – and pretty happy too. It would be marvellous, she thought, if they could stay there for ever. Why couldn't Geoffrey get a position in the local orchestra? They could get a lovely house overlooking the sea and be not only together, but acknowledged. But she knew he wouldn't. Even if he would have been content thus to buck the issue of his responsibilities, he wouldn't have given up his musical career. The American orchestras, he said, though good were not as good as the London ones, and American audiences were even more undiscriminating than English ones.

It was a pleasant interlude, but it was only an interlude. Sooner or later they would have to return to the reality of London – London in the winter! – and, as if to bring a foretaste of that reality, at the end of two weeks the MSO arrived to take their part in the festival. Their visit and the English Sinfonietta's would overlap by two days. And as if that were not enough, the hotel in which they were staying was the favourite with visiting musicians, and most of the Met Symf would be staying there too.

Annie hoped that at least Ted would be one of the musicians billeted elsewhere, though she had little hope of it; or that, if he was staying there, they would not actually meet, the schedules of the two orchestras not closely coinciding. Both hopes were doomed to disappointment. A brief enquiry at the desk revealed that E. Willment was one of the players booked in there, sharing a room with D. Bastowe. And on returning from a concert to dress for dinner on the evening that the MSO was arriving at Los Angeles airport, Annie and Geoffrey came into the hotel's foyer to find it full of musicians, suitcases and instruments.

'Oh God, just our luck,' Geoffrey muttered, rather restrainedly considering the circumstances. Annie was looking round and trying not to see, but a gap in the crowd presented her with the immediate sight of Ted, and their eyes met as if they had known where to look for each other. Her heart lurched. He looked very pale and tired, but otherwise just the same, just the same; his forelock falling forwards over his sad dark eyes, but his shoulders back in his almost military upright carriage in a way that looked strangely courageous.

There was only time for one brief stare, for the gap in the crowd closed again as quickly as it had opened, and Geoffrey, grabbing Annie's elbow, worked their way through the outermost edge of the bodies to the stairs, the access to the lifts being jammed with people, and they mounted to their room without further encounter.

They showered and dressed in silence, each occupied with private thoughts, and it was only as they prepared to leave for their evening engagement that Geoffrey spoke.

'Did you see him?' he said. Her eyes met his.

'Yes,' she said. 'He saw me, too.'

And that was all that was said on the subject.

162

# THIRTEEN

Annie and Geoffrey did not arrive back from the party until almost two in the morning, but as soon as they entered the foyer they could hear that some members of the orchestra were using the residents' privilege and having a night-of-arrival party.

'Noisy bastards,' Geoffrey said, rather amused. 'Shall we look in on them? It might be rather fun.'

'I don't think we should. I mean –'

'Come now, child, you're going to have to face up to each other sooner or later. You can't hope to avoid meeting this Wilmot bloke for ever.'

'Willment,' Annie corrected him doggedly, though she knew he only got the name wrong to annoy her.

'After all, we're all one big happy family in the music world – or hadn't you noticed. Better meet him with me to back you up, than meet him alone, don't you think?'

Annie wondered what he meant by that, for his look at her was rather sharp. Perhaps he thought she was in danger from him, that alone she might not be able to resist his charm. Some thought! Ted's charm was that he was totally undevious. No danger in that!

Geoffrey was obviously not going to be put off, so, apprehensively, she followed him into the bar. There were only about a dozen of the orchestra there, the two lady cellists and the rest were men, but they were making enough noise for twice their number, and they all appeared to be more or less sloshed. Ted was among them, and David Bastowe, as Annie noticed at once. A lull in the noise fell when Annie and Geoffrey entered, and Ted was heard to mutter something that sounded hostile, though the words were indistinct.

Geoffrey was greeted cheerfully, for only Ted's closest friends were likely to cut him for an escapade they would

163

rather like to have performed themselves, and only Ted and David and another couple of friends drew to one side and did not gather round the new arrivals. Annie followed Geoffrey unhappily, only too aware of how inflammatory their behaviour was, especially since everyone had been drinking.

'Hello, Geoffrey, how's the wife-snatcher?' Gordon Wilson greeted him. His eye went to Annie, slightly more coldly. 'How's tricks, Annie? Cor, you caused some problems running out on us like that – Tracy nearly had kittens trying to do your job for you. You'd better not show your face too often in certain quarters – you aren't the Most Popular Girl in the School, you know.'

Annie did not reply – there was nothing she could say – but Geoffrey took it in his stride. 'Shove it, Gordie,' he said. 'What's done's done, you know. Have a drink?'

'Got one, thanks. My shout, anyway – what're you having?'

'You're not going to buy that bugger a drink are you?' came a loud question from David Bastowe, propping up the bar further along. 'Tell him to go back to his own mob – if they'll have him. I don't know what the festival's coming to, hiring second-rate hacks like the ES. Why don't you tell him where to go, Gordie?'

'Oh shut up, Dave, you've had enough for one night,' Gordon replied without bothering to turn round. David turned his attention to Annie then.

'Here, Annie, Annie!' he called urgently. Annie kept her back rigidly turned. She didn't want to turn round and meet Ted's eye. Why did Geoffrey insist on this? It was too bad. It was in bad taste. 'Annie!' David went on. 'What's the matter – too grand for your old friends now, is that it? You've got a fortune on your back, I can see that. Was it worth it, what you did, for the nice dresses?'

'Shut up, David,' she heard Ted mutter. Geoffrey now no longer pretended to ignore what was going on. He turned lazily and regarded David with an insolent eye.

'What was that you were saying?' he asked.

'You mind your own business, you creep,' David shouted back belligerently.

Geoffrey, just as languidly, said, 'It is my business, when ladies are being insulted.'

'I don't see any ladies around,' David said, 'Only that blood-sucking flea that couldn't wait to swap dogs.'

Things happened quickly then. Geoffrey stepped forward to hit David, and as Annie swung round to try to stop him she met Ted's eye for a second and turned as red as if she'd been dipped in hot water before he swung a fist at David himself and floored his friend before Geoffrey had taken two steps towards him. David yipped like a trodden-on puppy, and sat down, putting his hand to his jaw and staring at Ted with puzzled, hurt eyes. Ted rubbed his knuckles with an agonised expression that would have made Annie laugh if it had been anyone else and for any other cause. Geoffrey glanced at Annie and shrugged, and turned away again, back to Gordon, putting out a hand to Annie to bring her into the group.

Ted gave Annie one long, last look before he bent over his fallen friend tenderly, saying, 'Come on, old son. You've had enough to drink. Time you went up to bed, I think.'

'What's got into you?' David asked as Ted helped him to his feet. 'Why the hell did you do that? It's that sod you should have been laying into, not me. I was only trying to help.'

'Never mind,' Ted said, soothingly. 'I'll fight my own battles. Come on, old son, let's get out of here. Let's go where the air is cleaner. I don't like the company we're keeping.'

Geoffrey put his arm round Annie's shoulder and drew her close while Ted and David walked past them and out of the bar, but she felt as if they were running hot irons across her back. She gave them long enough to get clear and then said to Geoffrey, 'Can we go now? I'd like to go to bed.'

'If you like. Come on then – good night, Gordon. Night, all.'

And they walked out of that, by now, fairly hostile atmosphere and went up the stairs to their room on the first floor.

But the events of the night were not yet over. They

165

undressed and got into bed, and Geoffrey had just put the lights out when there came a knocking on their door.

He put a finger to Annie's lips to tell her to be silent, and waited. The knocking came again, louder, and the door-knob was rattled.

'Who is it? Geoffrey called, slipping out of bed and reaching for his dressing-gown.

'Geoffrey – are you in there?' a voice called.

'Who is it?' Geoffrey said, approaching the door.

'It's me,' the voice said, and then, after a slight hesitation, 'Ted.'

'What do you want?' Geoffrey said, now standing by the door with his hand on the door-knob.

'I've got to talk to you,' Ted said.

'In the morning. Not now. Go away, go back to bed.'

There was a silence, and Annie thought he had obeyed and gone, but then there came another tentative knock, and the voice, more quietly.

'Is she there with you? Is she in there?'

'Go back to bed,' Geoffrey said again. There was a longer silence, and Geoffrey quietly opened the door and looked out into the corridor, then closed it and came back to bed.

'Has he gone?' she whispered.

'Out of sight,' Geoffrey said.

'I wonder what he wanted,' Annie said. Geoffrey lay down and pulled her down beside him.

'You, I should think,' he said. 'Go to sleep.'

It would have been easier said than done, except for the large quantity of liquor inside her, and the amount of dancing she had done.


Considering the delicate position they were in, Annie would have expected Geoffrey to keep her close by his side every minute, but when she woke the next morning she found he had gone off without waking her. There was a note in his neat, spiky handwriting under the travelling clock.

'You were sleeping so peacefully I didn't want to wake

you,' it said. 'No need for you to come to rehearsal this morning. Anyway, I've got some business to attend to. I'll meet you in the hotel coffee-shop at around one, and take you to lunch. G.'

She glanced at the clock – God, it was after eleven. She had slept like the dead. Showed she had needed it, anyhow. She decided to take a bath and then go and have a snack and some coffee, and read a book until one o'clock. In any case, you had to get in early if you wanted a seat in the coffee-shop at lunch-time. She'd be there before one and claim a place.

At ten past one Annie was still holding a place, rather guiltily as the tables around her filled up, and was spinning out cups of coffee. A flurried arrival made her look up with a greeting on her lips that died there when she saw it was not Geoffrey, but Ted, looking hot and bothered as if he had hurried to meet her there and known he was late.

'Hello,' she said at last, telling herself that this meeting was bound, as Geoffrey had said, to take place sooner or later.

'Hello,' he said. 'You're looking well.' His voice was strained, and she wondered if it was with suppressed emotion, or simply embarrassment.

'You're looking tired,' she said with truth. 'Actually, I'm saving this place.'

'Yes, I know. It's all right,' he said, sitting down. 'I knew you were here. I wanted to talk to you.' The waitress came to the table with the menu and a glass of iced water, and Ted waved the menu away distractedly and ordered coffee. When she had gone there was a silence during which Annie looked at him expectantly and he avoided her eyes. She felt most peculiar, not to say apprehensive. What might he be going to say, to ask?

'Well?' she said at last, unable to bear the silence any longer. He looked up unhappily.

'Annie,' he began, and then shrugged and gave a nervous smile. 'I don't know how to say what I want to say.' The waitress arrived with his coffee at that moment, and gave

167

him another breathing-space, but when she had left them alone again he did not seem any more eager to begin his speech, and Annie asked instead, 'Why did you come to the door last night?'

'I'm sorry about that. I was a bit drunk.'

'But what did you intend?'

'I suppose I just suddenly saw red. When he opened the door I was going to dash past him and snatch you away.'

Annie almost smiled at the idea, but thought better of it. 'On the principle that if one person can do it, so can another? Well, what changed your mind?'

'I realised in time that it was no answer. You're a grown woman, you can decide for yourself what you do and with whom. And suppose I'd done it and you'd let me? I'd never have known if it was what you wanted, or if you simply enjoyed being coerced.' This time Annie couldn't hide her smile, and he looked at her unhappily. 'Don't laugh. There are women like that.'

'I know,' Annie said. 'But I'm not one of them.'

'No?'

'No. Look, I want to tell you something. It may hurt you, or it may make things better, I don't know, but it's the truth. That night –' she hesitated, anxious not to use any words that might wound, 'the night I ran away, I was already going when Geoffrey came. I wasn't going to him – I just simply panicked, and then he turned up, and gave me somewhere to run to. So he didn't snatch me away.' She looked at him. 'I don't know if that makes it better or worse, but it's the truth.'

He nodded gravely. 'Thank you for telling me,' he said. 'I think perhaps it does help. At least then, it seems you didn't go through all that rigmarole simply to bring him to the point. To spite him.'

She was shocked. 'God, no! Is that what you thought? No, no, it wasn't that. I really did want to marry you, Ted, but when it came to it – I don't know. I was frightened I suppose. They say wedding-day nerves are rather common.'

'Then you did care for me a little?'

'I did. I do, I mean – why am I talking in the past tense? I do care for you. I was so sorry and ashamed when I'd done it – it was such a terrible thing to do. I don't suppose you could ever forgive me.'

'Do you want to be forgiven? Is that why you phoned me that night? It was you, wasn't it? I knew when I picked up the receiver, but you didn't speak. I wanted to tell you I wasn't angry, I wanted you to speak to me, but you put the phone down.'

'I was lonely,' she said quietly. 'I wanted to talk to you.' Their eyes met now, and his face was so familiar to her that it was almost as if she had met her own self face to face. It made her feel strange and happy and tearful all at once. It came to her suddenly that he was, after all, her husband, and that he was the one person in the world that she ought to feel like that about.

He reached across to touch her hand, and as she turned her palm upwards to receive the touch he closed his about it. His hand was warm and hard and dry, infinitely comforting.

'Annie,' he said, 'I told you I realised that you had to make your own decisions, so please don't think I'm here to bully you or coax you. You chose your own life, and I have no right to interfere with that. But I love you, and I just want to be sure that it is your choice, and that you're happy and don't regret it. To say that, if you wanted to come back to me, don't let pride or shame stand in your way. I'm here. I'll always be here.'

Annie swallowed hard. 'I don't regret it, Ted,' she said, and she saw the small hurt in his eyes in the fraction of a second before she went on, 'but that isn't because I'm happy. It seemed like an answer at the time, but –' she shrugged. 'We've managed to live without each other for so long that we've built up too much independence to share anything any more.' Ted pressed her hand. 'I still feel the same way about him. I think I always will. But I told you that, you knew how I felt about him.'

'You did. You were always honest with me. I admired that in you.'

She gave a small smile. 'You are a remarkable man. Most

men don't like honest women – they prefer to be lied to and comforted.'

'So – what happens now? You say it's not the answer?'

She shook her head. 'It was so good to be with him at first – like drinking cold water after a long hot dusty day. But then – it didn't go on. I was only a very small piece of his whole life, just as I always was. I couldn't have a life of my own or I'd never see him at all. And then – I suppose at last I had to admit to myself that I couldn't ever have my child back. Deep down I'd thought that somehow I could have him back and we could go back to being what we were, the three of us. But you can't go back. You can't ever go back. Not ever.'

She began to cry, quite quietly. Ted let go of her hand and stood up abruptly, aware of the proximity of other diners. 'Come on,' he said harshly. 'Let's walk.'

He came round the table and pulled her to her feet, and moments later they were out in the blessed privacy of the busy street, and walking fast while Annie's tears dried themselves. She found that Ted had hold of her hand again, and it was so comforting and right that she held onto it tightly like a child and let him lead her towards the park. They didn't speak again until they were sitting on a bench in a quiet corner, and Annie had recovered her composure. Then Ted took both her hands and made her look at him, and said in a firm voice from which he carefully schooled any emotion, 'Annie, I love you, and I want you back. That's *my* feelings, and nothing you have to worry about. If you want me to go, you only have to say so, and I will. I'll never trouble you again. But I want you to be happy, above all.' She opened her mouth to speak and he said nervously, 'You don't have to give me an answer now. I'm in no hurry.'

Afraid she was going to say no, she realised. She smiled at him, and he smiled back hesitantly, not knowing what her smile portended. She didn't have the words to carry her over the last obstacle, and perhaps he realised it, for after a moment he put his arms round her and drew her against him,

170

and with a sigh she rested her head on his shoulder and her cheek against his neck.

'Oh Ted,' she said, 'I'm so sorry.' She felt him freeze slightly at the words, and she hugged him harder to let him know it wasn't that. 'I'm so glad to be with you again,' she said. 'It's like coming home.'

A moment later she felt his body shaking slightly, and she held onto him tightly, tightly, her face hidden so that she should not have to see his tears.

A long time later, it seemed, she suddenly remembered, and thrust herself upright, staring at Ted, to say, 'Oh God, I've just realised – I was supposed to be meeting him in the coffee-shop! He'll be waiting there.'

'No, it's all right,' Ted said. 'I was talking to him this morning. That's how I knew where you were. I went to ask him how things were between you –'

'And what did he say?' Annie said in a low voice. Ted looked at her with a wry smile.

'Very much what you said. You *are* alike, you know, you and him. He said that he felt just the same about you, that he had always loved you and always will, but that for him just to know you are in the same world is enough.' She turned her head away slightly as the old feelings rushed over her again. 'He said he thought you weren't happy, and that I should speak to you and offer you the choice, so he sent me to meet you instead of him. He said – he said to tell you that he'll never change.'

Annie nodded, still looking away. She knew what he meant by that – that his feelings would never change, that he would always love her just as he did, and that his habits and wants and lifestyle would never change either. Giving her her freedom, as far as she or he could ever be free of each other. The unfinished business between them would always remain unfinished, because there was nothing either of them could do about it, about chance, about the past, about their own natures.

'He gave me everything I have, he made me what I am,' she said. It sounded like a tribute to the dead. You can't go back,

171

not ever, not ever. She looked at Ted, looked into his kind, all-loving, all-understanding eyes, felt the warmth of his regard for her, the lambent clarity of his integrity that would never encroach on her independence of mind. 'I am your wife,' she said. It was his answer. He said, 'I think he knew what you would say. He said you were crying in your sleep last night.'

By unspoken consent they got up and began to walk again. 'What a lot of trouble I've caused everybody,' she sighed. 'I'll never be able to face people again.'

'They'll forget before you do,' he said. 'Five-minute wonder. And they won't dare say anything to your face. Unless of course you run away and leave me again.'

'Not again,' she said. 'Pat said it was about time I stopped running. I think he's right.'

'A very sensible bloke, Pat; and very fond of you.'

'You know about Pat and me? And you understand?'

'I understand everything about you. You can trust me, don't you know that?' She nodded. 'Perhaps you'll stop running away from your music too, now. You know why you stopped playing, don't you?'

He really did understand, then. 'I'll try,' she said. 'But it isn't important any more.'

'Then it bloody well should be. None of that defeatist talk, woman! What are you going to do with your life otherwise – clean floors?'

They walked on, talking pleasantly. Strange how their happiness took such a quiet form. No violent outburst of joy, no passionate kiss – they simply and quietly took up their relationship where it had been broken off.

'Do you know where we are?' he asked her suddenly. She shook her head. 'A block from the back door of our hotel.'

She stared at him, and a grin spread slowly over his face. 'You cunning bastard,' she said. 'You arranged that deliberately, didn't you?'

'Me? Deliberately? Perish the thought! But still, since we are here, wouldn't you like to come up to my room for a bit?'

'What an offer! But won't the management object?'

'How can they? We are married, after all,' he said. 'It's nice that we won't have to go through all that again, though on the other hand it would have been nice to have some way of showing the world what you mean to me.'

In the lift it all came over her in great waves and she put herself into his arms and pressed her face against him.

'I want you like crazy, you lovely man,' she said, muffled by his cheek. 'I feel as if I want to climb right inside you and hide myself away. Love me a lot, won't you, and for a long, long time. I don't think I could bear it if anything were to go wrong with us after this.'

The lift doors opened, and they walked calmly the few steps to his room, and were inside, and in each others arms again.

'I'll never leave you,' he said. 'Not ever. I'll love you until we both die, and if there's any life after death, I'll go on loving you through that, too. How can I prove it to you? Do you really doubt me?'

'No, I know you mean it. You don't have to prove it. Just go on loving me. And –' she hesitated, and he put her back to arm's length to look at her.

'What?' he said. 'You can say anything to me, don't be afraid. What is it?'

Her grey eyes looked up into his brown ones, seeking confirmation, looking for the assurance that she could trust him.

'There is just one thing you could do for me.'

'What?'

'Give me children. I want a baby.'

He was shaking, and he wondered if his legs were going to give way, but he held her at arm's length for a moment longer so that she could read his face. Then he pulled her to him again, and closed his eyes against the flood tide of feelings that threatened to break him.

'Lots of them,' he said at last, huskily. 'As many as you like. All you have to say is when.'

'When,' she said.